Catching Kate

novella

D. KELLY

Dedication

This book is dedicated to my husband and kids. Without them, my life would be boring and unexceptional. There is never a day that passes that I'm not thankful for their unyielding faith and love. I love you guys with all my heart and soul.

Catching Kate

What the heart has once owned and had, it shall never lose. ~ Henry Ward Beecher

Part One

Every Ending has a Beginning

I can't sleep. I've been lying here since Connor came back from checking on Kate at the gym. *Kate,* she's *my* Katherine, and she's even more breathtaking now than ever before. I have so many emotions flowing through me at the moment. The strongest of them all is heartbreak. I didn't think it was possible to feel any more pain, until I saw her. Watching her pull inside herself, effectively distancing her emotions from us, was excruciatingly painful. I don't want her to feel toward me the same way she feels about Joseph. All I wanted to do was pull her into my arms and tell her how much I've missed her, how much I love her, and how *nothing* in my life has made sense ever since I pushed her away.

I may lose my family, all of them, because of this self-inflicted clusterfuck I've created. Daniel, Connor, and Jake are my best friends, my brothers. Jess and Kate were my *everything* before this, and now everyone I love is wrapped up in this mess.

It's not like I don't know I fucked up, of course I know that. It's going to take perseverance, time, and a whole lot of groveling to get Kate to even *think* about taking me back. I'm prepared for the fight of my life. Even though she has someone else, it shouldn't be that *hard* to win her back. What we were, what we *are*, is impenetrable. I know it'll take some time for her to realize we're what's best for each other. I told her in the letter I would honor a relationship if she was in one. I didn't mean it. I know that makes me a dick, but I honestly never even thought it would be necessary. Our love is stronger than anything else she could have possibly found. I've been flailing for years without her, so I figured she had been, too. I didn't expect her to welcome me with open arms, but I'm ready to fight—fight for her, and for my place in her life, and most definitely for my place in her heart.

I'm pissed off—no, I'm *beyond* pissed—I'm fucking *furious* that Daniel is the one. Even if I haven't heard it from her, I've heard it from him. He's my brother, my savior, and the guy Kate is currently fucking. Just thinking about it makes my blood boil. She's mine, damn it, and no one should know what fucking her feels like except for me. That's not exactly true, though, I never *fucked* Kate. I *made love* to her. I've been fucking all these random women ever since, but they've never meant anything to me. Daniel's had her both ways—he's made love to her *and* he's fucked her. The fact that I know *those* details about *them* torments my soul in unimaginable ways.

I'm jealous as hell. I know it's not his fault. I never said anything to anyone. I never gave her last name, never showed anyone the pictures that have been shoved under my bed. I never told anyone how beautiful I thought she was the first time we met, even though we were only seven years old. I never told a soul that watching her lose her mom broke a piece of me off that I'll never get back. That piece of me is the piece of my soul that I gave to her. It's the piece that our entire friendship and relationship grew from. It's the purest part of my heart that was meant for her and only her.

I never told them that the first time we kissed I knew I could never be serious about anyone else, even though we were only in seventh grade. I didn't tell them how before I asked her to be my girlfriend I threw up. Nobody knows that the night we made love for the first time I was so nervous that I threw up...again. They have no clue that when it was over, I cried in the shower like a pussy because I was so overwhelmed by it all. I never said how utterly in love I was, and how at eighteen years old, I was wishing for babies instead of college. Nobody knows any of it, because if I would've talked about her... that would have been admitting that I lost the best part of me. Willingly.

There's no way I'm going to accept that. I know I fucked up. I know with absolute certainty that this entire mess is one hundred percent my fault. I don't even blame my mom anymore; the decision was mine, and mine alone. I'm positive that as much as *I* feel like an asshole right now, it probably doesn't even *begin* to describe how much of an asshole my friends think I am. Fuck, if I would've never ditched town on her birthday and just gone to Connor's party, none of this would even be happening.

How is it even possible that she fell in love with him in *two weeks*? We knew each other almost our entire lives and I was so nervous trying to propose that night. I let the moment slip through my fingers a few times before it was too late and I missed it altogether. In two weeks, Daniel gets her to fall in love and promise herself to him, leaving me in the dust. What the fuck?

In my heart I know he deserves to be happy. Kate makes him happier than I've ever seen him in all the years I've known him. I *want* him to be happy. He deserves a lifetime of happiness and love with a girl who feels the same. It just can't be *my* girl, he can't have Kate. I won't willingly stand back and let this happen and that makes me the biggest asshole on the planet. Daniel saved me. Without him, who knows where I would be right now? And I'm going to pay him back by taking his girl. *My girl.*

After we see Kate, I need to talk to Daniel. If I'd tried tonight, we would've come to blows and that's the last thing I want. If I can get him to listen to our story from the day I met her until the bitter end maybe he could understand she belongs with me. Understand that she owns my soul, that there isn't a piece of my heart that doesn't belong to her. He doesn't have to like it, but if he can see that this is so much more than Kate being my ex-girlfriend, it might go a long way toward saving our friendship.

Since I'm not going to get any sleep tonight, I might as well think of the best way to explain it all to him. Going back to the beginning would be the best place to start...

Chapter 1 ~ Back to the Beginning
Michael ~ 7 years old

"Michael, are you okay back there, buddy? You're awful quiet today… I know you weren't looking forward to moving again, but I promise this *is* the last time for a long time." *That's what he said last time and the time before.*

"I'm fine, just hoping there are some kids in this neighborhood, Dad." My dad blows air from his mouth; he does that when he's trying not to get mad at me. It's not *my* stupid fault we're moving again. It sucks not having any friends.

"We're only around the corner from Joseph, buddy. He has a daughter your age and she's in the same grade. I told you about her. Her name is Katherine. We're going over there for dinner tonight so you can meet her."

"But, Dad, she's a *girl*! I don't *want* to be friends with a stupid girl! I want to play *baseball* not *Barbies*. Why did we have to move again? I finally had friends."

"I get it, bud, I do, but you have to trust that your mother and I are doing this with your best interests in mind. This isn't like last time, or the time before that. This time we own half of the company, and one day, when you grow up, you can work with your old man."

Yeah right. "Nope, I'm gonna be a catcher for the Dodgers, not be stuck inside with grown-ups all day." *Great, now he's laughing at me and it's not funny.*

"Michael, if you play for the Dodgers I'll be at every game I can, but if that doesn't work out I've got an office next to mine ready for you. Just trust me, this time *will* be different. I don't want you to worry; this is going to be home for a long time. It's a much nicer house than our last one, not as big as Joseph's, but close."

The houses on this street *are* really big, a lot bigger than our other house. I watch two girls get out of a car as we pass by but don't see any other kids playing outside. None. I bet this neighborhood has nothing but stupid girls in it. I don't see a park anywhere, either, which means I can't ride my bike to the baseball field. This place sucks.

We park in front of a big white house and my mom's car is in the driveway. It's bigger than our last house but there are no kids on this street, either. At least those girls are just around the corner. Maybe they have brothers I can play with. It's not too far to ride my bike; my mom will let me go a couple of streets over.

"Come on, Michael, let me show you the house before we go to dinner. We've got a surprise inside I think you'll like."

The house looks a lot like our old house inside and my mom is pretty happy about that. "Michael, all of your things are already in your new room. Why don't you run upstairs and see if you can figure out which room is yours? We'll be up in a minute."

I take off running up the stairs as fast as I can. Right at the top is a big playroom just for me! There are action figures, video games, a TV, and a big couch; maybe it won't be so bad not having a park close by. My room looks the same but bigger, *way* bigger, and I even have my own bathroom. This is awesome. My dad wasn't lying.

"Well, buddy, what do you think?"

"It's really cool!"

"Your mom thought you might really like to have a place to bring friends over and hang out." *What friends?*

"If I *make* any new friends. This still sucks."

"Give it time, buddy, you'll make more friends than you know what to do with. Come on, let's go to dinner and meet some right now."

"Okay."

The house we pull up to looks like the house those girls were at earlier. This house is a lot bigger than our house—they must be *really* rich! A very pretty lady with reddish hair answers the door and lets us in; she looks nice. "You must be Michael. We've heard so much about you. My name is Lila. I'm Katie Grace's mom." Lila places a gentle hand on my shoulder and calls for the girls. "Katie Grace, Jessica, come meet Michael and then you can all go up and play."

They're the girls I saw earlier. The one with reddish hair talks first, "Hi, Michael, I'm Katherine but everyone calls me Katie Grace, and this is my best friend Jessica. Want to come play *Super Smash Brothers* with us?" *Cool girls that play video games? Maybe this won't be so bad.*

"Yeah, sure, I like that game." Jessica smiles, she's the one with the black hair but she hasn't said anything yet. Katherine motions for me to follow them. She's pretty... for a girl...too bad girls have cooties. Oh well, we're just playing video games—it's not like I'm gonna kiss her or anything.

Chapter 2 ~ When she falls

"Hey, Jessica, what are we getting on our pizza tonight? I want pepperoni and sausage." Jessica rolls her eyes at me. She just learned how to do that and she does it all the time when she's annoyed, or trying to act like she doesn't care, or whatever. Chloe said she's going to smack her if she doesn't stop. She probably will, too, because Chloe is super mean to Jessica.

"Sausage is nasty, I want peppers."

Pizza is supposed to be full of meat. Then again, at least she doesn't want anchovies...I don't know why *anyone* would want those. "Peppers are nasty, why do you always want vegetables and fruit on your pizza?"

"Whatever, Michael. Katie's going to want peppers, too, you know she will."

I glare at her but finally agree, "Fine, we'll get pepperoni and peppers."

A huge smile breaks across Jessica's face. Who knew peppers could make her that happy? "You like her. I *knew* it, but now I *know* it! You like Katie!"

That's why she's smiling. What the heck? "I do not!"

"You do too. If you didn't like her you wouldn't have given up your sausage so easily."

Now I roll my eyes at her. "It's called majority rule, stupid. There are two of you and one of me, so you guys win."

"Um, guys?"

Oh great, how much of that did Katie Grace hear? I don't want her to think I like her. I mean, I guess she's cute for a girl, but she's my best friend, so... yuck. "Hey, Katie Grace," I answer, but my eyes are glued to my shoes.

"My mom's almost ready, so we're going to head to your house as soon as they leave. I had an idea for the pizza...you know, we can get all pepperoni but half with peppers and half with sausage—that would be perfect for all of us." *Yup, she heard us. She's blushing and acting kind of shy. That's just great.*

"That sounds good, doesn't it, Michael?"

"Um, yeah, that sounds good. Thanks, guys." I finally look up and Katie Grace is smiling, not really *at* me, just in general. That's a relief.

"Kids, go wait by the front door, please, we're getting ready to leave," Maryanne calls to us from the entryway. Tonight is going to be fun. We're eating pizza, playing video games, and having a sleepover in my loft. Our parents are all going to some charity dinner that Lila is really excited about. Katie Grace said her mom has been really sad lately, but the past few days she's been really excited about this dinner. That's a good thing because her dad is kind of a big jerk. When Lila is sad, Katie Grace is sad, and I don't like it when Katie Grace is sad.

We're all waiting at the bottom of the stairs for Lila and Katie Grace. Maryanne had Katie Grace run a bottle of ibuprofen up to her because she had a headache. Whenever the grown-ups go out it always takes forever for them to leave. Girls take forever with all their dresses, hair, makeup and high heels. Yeah, they look pretty, but they look pretty in just regular clothes, too, and the rest of us don't have to wait so long for them. Jessica doesn't seem to care, though. She's bouncing up and down with excitement.

"I can't wait to see how Lila looks tonight! She always looks so pretty. I bet Katie Grace is going to look just like that when we get older." Jessica looks excited and sad at the same time.

"She probably will and you'll probably look just like Chloe. I'll probably look like my dad—that's just how it works."

She shakes her head, "I don't think so, Michael. You already look more like your mom and I'll never be lucky enough to be pretty like Chloe."

Stupid Chloe. She's so mean to Jessica, always calling her fat. She's not fat. My mom says she's pleasantly plump and that it wouldn't matter if she was fat because she's beautiful inside and out. Too bad Jessica doesn't believe it.

"Jessica, you *are* pretty like Chloe. So what if you're not starving yourself all the time to be skinny. Chloe is mean and you're not. She's probably mean because she's hungry. I know when I'm hungry I can be mean. Don't listen to her. None of us believe the crap she says to –you, so neither should you."

She raises her sad blue eyes to mine and nods, "Thanks, Michael. I'm so glad you're not a jerk like those other boys in our class." I nod my head at her, but before I say anything else, Lila and Katie Grace finally come down the stairs. They're both smiling but Lila's doesn't seem as happy as Katie Grace's. Maybe it's because her head is still hurting.

All the grown-ups start gushing about how nice they all look. They do look nice but I wish they would hurry up and leave. I'm starving. I haven't eaten since my baseball game earlier. My dad and Joseph give my mom and Lila kisses. At least they're on the cheek; it's so gross when they kiss on the mouth. My dad says someday I'll be excited to kiss a girl like that but I don't think so.

"Okay, kids, remember the rules. Listen to Maryanne, clean up your messes, no scary movies, and in bed by midnight. Got it?" We nod at them with a chorus of "Yes, Moms" and "Yes, Lilas"

"Katie Grace, come and give me a hug since I won't see you until tomorrow. I love you." Katie Grace gives her a big hug - she's so close with her mom; I wish Chloe could be like that. "I love you, too, Mom."

"I love you more"

Katie Grace giggles, "No, Mom, I love *you* more."

Lila smiles a real smile this time. "Impossible, Katie Grace, I love you with all the love I've ever had to give. I love you more than the whole wide world." Katie Grace is still giggling as Lila finishes kissing her cheek and turns to get her coat.

Suddenly, as Lila reaches for her coat, she starts to fall. She must have slipped in those high heels. Katie Grace screams, "MOM!" as Joseph and my dad catch Lila right before she hits the floor. Everyone is rushing around, and Maryanne is calling an ambulance, but I barely notice the adults. Katie Grace is on the floor next to Lila crying, screaming, "Mommy, wake up! Mommy, *please* wake up! Dad, wake her up. WAKE HER UP!"

My mom and Maryanne pull her away but she's kicking and screaming. Jessica clutches my hand hard and she has tears running down her face. I'm glued to the spot I'm standing in, just watching everything going on around me. I've never seen someone's skin change color before, but I could've sworn that a few seconds ago, Lila wasn't white like she is now.

I don't know what to do. Katie Grace won't stop screaming and Jessica won't stop squeezing the crap out of my hand. I feel like I should be doing *something* like the grown-ups are doing. I pull Jessica over to Katie Grace. Jessica let's go of my hand, sits next to her, and hugs her something fierce. I sit down, hugging hug her from behind and continue to look over my shoulder at what's going on. I know I shouldn't be staring, but I want to see when she wakes up. The paramedics are here now checking her out. I don't understand anything that they're saying even though I hear every word.

"Left pupil is blown, right pupil is fixed and dilated. Her pulse is weak and thready. Let's get her on the gurney... we have to go now. IV is in, pushing fluids."

My mom takes control of the situation. "Maryanne, drive with Grant to the hospital and take Katie Grace. I'll take the kids to my house. Joseph needs to go with the ambulance..."

My mom's orders are cut off by a loud beeping noise as the paramedics are pushing the gurney through the door. "No pulse, initiating CPR now!" One of the firemen jumps in and pushes the gurney as the paramedic jumps on Lila, pushing up and down on her chest and breathing into her mouth. It's scary to watch, and now all the grown-ups are crying too.

Maryanne and Dad got Katie Grace in the car and took off behind the ambulance. Jessica is squeezing my hand again, but I'm so scared I almost don't feel it. "Kids, I'm going to go lock things up and then we'll head over to our house. I know you're scared, so am I, but it's all going to be okay. Please wait here, don't move, I'll be right back."

After my mom leaves, Jessica looks at me with tears still streaming down her cheeks. "Do you think she's going to be okay, Michael?" I look at her and shrug my shoulders. *She was so white when they left.* "I don't know, Jessica, but I hope so."

We got to my house about fifteen minutes after the ambulance left for the hospital. My mom ordered our pizza even though none of us are hungry anymore. Jessica and I are watching TV in the loft, well not watching, but it's on while my mom waits for the pizza downstairs. I heard the phone ring a minute ago, maybe it's my dad with some good news about Lila. I know soon enough that isn't the case when I hear my mom sobbing. Jessica and I look at each other, neither of us moving, but we're both crying, too.

It takes a few minutes, but my mom finally comes upstairs and sits between Jessica and me. Wrapping an arm around each of us, she explains as gently as she can that Lila went to Heaven. All I can think about is how happy Katie Grace was when Lila told her she loved her, and now she doesn't have a mom anymore. That makes me really cry hard. Boys aren't supposed to cry, they're supposed to be strong. I try to wipe my tears away but they keep coming.

"Michael, it's okay to cry and be sad. Boys don't have to be strong all the time. Sometimes in life, sadness trumps everything; it's *okay* to feel your emotions. Never try and hide them or change that, kiddo." I hug my mom even tighter.

"Mom, what happens now that Lila's gone?" My mom looks at me and starts crying again. "Well, I guess Katie Grace has to get used to spending more time with Joseph and depending on him for things that Lila used to do for her." *Yeah, that won't happen... even I know that.*

"Mom...Do you think you can be Katie Grace's mom, too? I don't mind sharing you. She's a girl and she needs a mom, not a dad. Well, she needs a dad, too, but you know what I mean, right?" There is a shimmer in my mom's eyes; she looks extremely proud and sad all at the same time.

"Michael, you're such an amazing kid. I can help Katie Grace, *if* she wants me to. She's welcome here anytime and we'll include her in all of our family things, too, from now on." She turns her head to Jessica and pulls her in closer. "You too, sweetie. Anytime you want, you feel free to come, too. You *both* are welcome here anytime. I could never be a replacement for Lila in Katie Grace's life, Michael, but I would be happy to treat her like my own child when she's around."

That makes me feel better. I think it makes Jessica feel better, too, because she's not crying anymore, either.

"Claire, can we go see Katie Grace now?"

My mom shakes her head, "Sorry, Jessica, I know you guys want to be there for your friend, but she needs time with Joseph right now... alone. Maryanne is going to pick you up after she drives them home. Tomorrow, we'll all go over and help Joseph and Katie Grace, with whatever they need, but tonight they need to be together. Maryanne said the doctor was sending Katie Grace home with something to help her sleep, she was very upset at the hospital." I swear my mom flinched when she said that. I bet she's thinking that Joseph isn't going to be any help for Katie Grace. I also bet we head over there bright and early tomorrow morning.

~~~***~~~

I didn't sleep much last night. I've never had anyone die before and I'm glad because this sucks. I tried to get Katie Grace on the walkie talkies last night but she must have been sleeping. Jessica was up, though, so we talked for a while. Lila bought us these really far range walkie talkies so we could all have missions in the neighborhood. Lila had the fourth one so she could be our commander and send us out on scavenger hunts and stuff. She was so much fun; I already miss her so much. It's barely light outside but I can't sleep. I want to see if my parents are up and if we can go to Katie Grace's yet. I can't stop thinking about her. I'm sad about Lila, but when I think about Katie Grace missing Lila... that's when the tears come back. I really just want to see if she's okay, I know *I* wouldn't be.

My mom and dad are sitting at the table, holding hands, and drinking their coffee. Neither of them looks like they got much sleep. "Michael, what are you doing up so early, sweetheart?" My mom pulls me into a hug and kisses the top of my head.

I make sure and hug her back hard; I don't want to ever lose her. "I couldn't sleep and I kept trying to get Katie Grace to talk to me on the walkie talkies and she didn't answer. Can we go see if she's okay now...*please?*"

My parents exchange one of those parent looks and motion for me to sit down. My dad is the first one to speak up, "Buddy, I know you're worried about Katie Grace, we all are. What you have to understand is that..."

My dad gets choked up and my mom continues for him, "Sweetie, you just need to know that she's going to need time, possibly lots of time, and she still might not be the same girl she was before. I know this is difficult to understand, but death changes people. Losing her mother at such a young age is not just unbelievably sad; it's a life changing event."

My stomach drops like I'm on a roller coaster. *They have no idea what they're talking about.*

"No, Mom, you don't understand. Katie Grace is going to be fine; I'm going to make sure of it. She's my best friend and I won't let her *not* be fine. I'll fix her, Mom. I'll do whatever I can to make her happy and not let her be sad. I'll fix her, I promise! Can we go now, please, can we just go?"

My mom nods her head but she's crying again. "Okay, buddy, go get dressed and we'll leave in about a half hour." After I round the corner, I hear my mom sobbing so I stop, wondering if I should go back. "Grant, was she really that bad? I don't know if we can take him over there if she was that bad. Why did they let Joseph take her home? Don't you think they should have kept her at the hospital?"

I hear my dad shhshhhing my mom. "It was bad, Claire. I've never seen anything like it. Katie Grace was nearly catatonic. For the longest time she was just crying silently and suddenly this gut-wrenching sob came out of her. She fell to the floor and screamed like a wounded animal. It was understandable, but when we tried to pick her up and comfort her, she lashed out at everyone. You would have thought we were kidnapping her. She was kicking and screaming and crying out for Lila to help her."

I take a seat on the steps and listen, my dad's voice cracking as he speaks "Eventually, they came in and gave her a shot to calm her down. The nurse said that it was just to relax her, but that's when she became almost catatonic. The nurse was concerned about her reaction and got the doctor, but Joseph insisted she not be admitted. He told them she needed to mourn in private. Immediately after we got her settled at home, Joseph started removing all the pictures of Lila in the house. Joseph said, and I quote 'Katherine does not need any reminders of what happened today.' I don't know, Claire, I think that's only going to make everything worse, but I'm not a shrink."

"Oh, that isn't going to help *anything*! He can't just take away all the reminders of her mother. What is he thinking? I think Michael has the right idea. Let's get over there and monitor things. The sooner the better, before he loses his ever loving mind and does something he'll regret."

I hurry and go get dressed. I need to see Katie Grace now more than ever. My heart hurts thinking about what my parents said about how she could change. She's my best friend, even more than Jessica. We've always had a very special connection and I'm not going to lose her. I'm going to fight and make sure she comes back to us like her normal self. Once I'm dressed, I grab my giant teddy bear that I won at the fair and take it downstairs. Katie Grace loves this bear more than I do. She hugs it and cuddles with it every time she comes over.

"I'm ready, can we go now?" My parents look up at me and nod.

"Sure, buddy, let's go. What's with the bear?" I roll my eyes. *What's with the stupid question? They should know what it's for.* "I'm giving him to Katie Grace. He should cheer her up—she loves Wally." My parents exchange one of those parental looks but I don't care.

I remember the day I won him on the way to her house.

We were at the Ventura County Fair and the guy running the booth's name was Wally. Wally could see how much we wanted to win the bear and he told us it was his last day working at the carnival. He had gotten a better job, closer to his family, and he was really excited about it. Every time we missed the bucket he gave us more balls. Katie Grace only made one whiffle ball into the basket the entire time, but after about an hour, I had gotten enough in that Wally gave me the bear. I asked Katie Grace if she wanted him, but she just shook her head and said that she was just going to keep playing carnival games until she could beat the pants off me. When we got him home, she said she thought we should name him Wally, and he would be a reminder of not only someone who was kind to us, but also for us to be kind to others, too.

Joseph answers the door when we arrive. He looks bad; you can tell he didn't sleep last night, either. When he sees I have Wally he almost cracks a smile. "Michael, Katherine is still sleeping, but if you want to go wait in her loft until she wakes up and watch some television, go ahead." I nod my head at him and race up the stairs faster than I ever have before. I knock lightly on her door but she doesn't answer. I tiptoe inside and place Wally on the bed next to her. She opens her eyes immediately. *She doesn't look like she was sleeping.*

"Sorry, Katie Grace, I didn't mean to wake you up." She doesn't say a word, just shakes her head no. "I didn't wake you up?" She shakes her head no again. I guess she doesn't want to talk. Maybe her throat hurts from all the crying.

"Do you want me to get you some water? Does your throat hurt?" She shakes her head again and points to her heart. *Oh God.* "I'm so sorry. I know you miss her. I promise somehow I'll help you make your heart feel better." Silent tears fall from her sad, murky eyes that are usually so green and bright.

I look around for some tissues but there aren't any, so I wipe her tears off with my fingers. The whole time she just looks at me with a blank stare. Eventually, she rolls over and hugs Wally. She doesn't move for a long time, but I sat there on the floor next to her bed anyway. I'm not going anywhere. After maybe an hour, she gets up to use the restroom and I take my chance to move up to the bed to be closer to her.

When she comes back, she sits next to me, leaning up against the wall, hugging her knees to her chest and starts sobbing. Listening to her cry like that forever wounds my heart. I'll do anything I can to try and stop her pain. "Don't cry, Katie Grace. Please don't cry." I put my arm over her shoulder; it feels weird but also strangely good. I pull her into me and rest my head against hers. "What can I do, Katie Grace? Please, tell me what I can do to help you."

She jerks away from me and through her hiccupping and sobbing she finally answers me. "Don't ever call me that again. My name is Katherine, my mom called me Katie Grace and now she's gone. DON'T EVER CALL ME KATIE GRACE AGAIN!" After screaming at me, she grabs Wally and flops back on the bed. I don't know how much time passed, but she cried herself back to sleep. I've never heard her yell before. Ever. I know it's because she's sad, and for the first time, I wonder if I'm going to be able to bring her back to us after all.

~~~***~~~

Over the next few days not much changed. I continued to sit by her bedside two days in a row. The third day was the funeral, and by then she had at least stopped crying, if only temporarily. The funeral was sad, really, *really* sad. Through the whole thing Katherine held on to my hand like it was her life preserver. There wasn't anyone there who didn't cry, how could there be? Lila was the nicest person any of us ever knew. I was the only one she would allow to touch her. Jessica tried, but it was as if she just couldn't have contact with more than one person at a time. *I* was her person. For some reason it made my heart puff up in my chest like something you would see in a cartoon. Katherine hadn't really spoken to anyone except for me in three days. By that point, people were starting to freak out. I wasn't too worried, though. She was in there sorting things out in her head. It was *her* way, the way *she* needed to deal with what happened.

When the priest asked if anyone wanted to say a few words about Lila, a few people went up. But after the last person spoke, Katherine decided she needed to say something. I don't think any of us were the same walking out of that funeral as we were when we walked into it, not after hearing her speak. In between her words she was crying silent tears.

"My name is Katherine Grace Moore. Most people call me Katie Grace. I don't *ever* want to hear anyone call me Katie Grace again. That name belongs to my mom. I don't know why I only got her for ten years when she was so amazing. My mom made us scavenger hunts and bought us walkie talkies. She took me to gymnastics and baked us cookies. She made the best sleepover forts and she had the smile of an angel. I think God must have missed her smile and missed her spirit because I can't think of any other reason he would take her from us. When she...when my mom...right before she fell...right before she...she...died...

Katherine pulls the microphone out of the podium while crying and sits on the ground, pulling her knees up to her chest, sobbing violently. Maryanne tried to get her to go sit back down but she wouldn't move. My heart was racing the entire time; every piece of me needed to go rescue her, but my dad put his hand firmly in my lap and shook his head at me so I knew better. I didn't like it, though. She needed me and I was so close and still couldn't help her. Then it was like she got a second wind. She wiped the tears off her face with the back of her hand but remained seated.

"When my mom died, she had just finished telling me how much she loved me. She let me know that all the time. I know my mom loved me, but I wonder if I didn't know…if she wouldn't have said it all the time…if God would have still taken her. Maybe if I didn't know he would have let her stay until I understood. If I could have her back, I would pretend to never understand how much she loved me so that God would let me keep her. She was the best mom and I don't know what I'm going to do without her. Since you're all here, she must have loved you, too. I'm sorry you have to feel how I'm feeling. It hurts so much. I don't know how to fix it and… I'm so sorry… I can't fix you all, either."

After that, I think the whole church was in tears, including Joseph. Maryanne tried to take Katherine but she wasn't having it; she came and sat right next to me. She grabbed my hand and her head rested on my shoulder while she cried all her tears on my new suit.

When we buried Lila, Katherine lost it all over again, but this time she was still holding on to me. I hugged her back with all I had to give and cried with her. Once, I watched this show on prides of lions and how they protect each other from predators. Sitting there with Katherine and Jessica, watching my two best friends cry, makes me feel like I'm in a lion pride. I hate seeing them like this; I feel like I need to fix it somehow. Even more importantly, I want to fix it. From now on, I vow to be like a male in the pride and make sure they always stay safe and protected.

A few weeks after the funeral, Katherine started feeling a little better and decided it was time to go back to school. She said it was what Lila would have wanted. We go to a private school with lots of other rich kids. We're kind of like the Three Musketeers and don't hang out with the other kids much—they act like jerks. Jessica gets made fun of because of her weight a lot. I get made fun of because I hang out with two girls. Luckily, Katherine is so nice to everyone that she never gets made fun of. At least she didn't before Lila died.

On Katherine's first day back to school, we ran into Bryce Patterson at lunch. Bryce's dad is one of the richest guys in the world, at least that's what Bryce tells everyone. It's probably true because the school lets him get away with everything. Two months ago, he broke into the science lab and set it on fire. No one got hurt, but they're still rebuilding that section of the school. Bryce didn't even get suspended. We try and stay away from him because he's super mean to Jessica. Unfortunately for us, today the sixth graders are celebrating and get two lunch periods, so he's out on the playground with the fifth graders.

"Well, look what we have here, if it isn't fat ass and her posse."

I push my way in front of the girls. "Shut it, Bryce, we don't need your crap."

Bryce laughs his evil snicker, "What are *you* going to do about it, pansy?"

I move even closer to him; I'm so tired of his crap. "I'm not going to let you talk to my friends like that. Back off."

"Look, Matthews, you're a pansy and I'm not afraid of you. Your only friends are fat ass over here and the homely motherless girl. That's right, Katie, you've always been a freak but now you're a freak without a mom. From now on, you three are going to be fat ass, pansy, and motherless freak."

Bryce starts laughing and Katherine starts crying, which only makes Bryce laugh harder. As for me, that prideful lion feeling comes over me and I throttle Bryce with everything I have. I'm so glad I know how to fight. My dad's been taking me to the boxing gym with him since I was five. We go every weekend and Bryce is about to feel it.

I'm on top of Bryce and it probably looks like the fight scene from *A Christmas Story* to anyone that is watching us. In between punches, I'm telling him what's going to happen.

"You asshole, you're done making fun of us. No more fat ass, no more pansy, never again. And if I *ever* hear you say one word to Katherine about not having a mom again, I *will* kill you. Never call her Katie, either, asswipe, it's Katherine." By this time, blood is squirting out of Bryce's nose and he's crying. *Stupid jerk makes fun of people and doesn't even know how to fight.* The teachers pull us apart and escort all of us to the office. My heart's pounding. Katherine and Jessica look shocked, but I wasn't going to let him talk about Katherine like that. Jessica can hold her own. She usually tells Bryce where to stick it herself.

They called our parents and put all of us and our parents in the office to talk it out. Guess what? Bryce's mom...yeah, she's not exactly skinny. *This will work out good for us. I bet she isn't going to like hearing what her son calls Jessica.*

First, Bryce gives his story and makes it sound like I beat him up for no reason after telling Katherine he was sorry about her mom. Then he and his parents just sit there looking smug.

Katherine and Jessica said he was making fun of us and I stood up for them. They didn't mention what he said, but I wasn't about to hold back.

When it's my turn, I tell them *everything*. All the fat ass comments, the pansy comments, *and* the dead mom stuff. Bryce's parents don't look so smug anymore. Jessica and Katherine confirmed my story and Bryce was suspended. I didn't get off easy, though; I got suspended, too. But after that day, Bryce never bothered any of us again.

Chapter 3 ~ First Kisses and Friendship ~ The Teenage Years

Today is Katherine's birthday and she's having a party. It's going to be fun, and after the party, Jessica and I are spending the night. Maryanne bought us the entire *Nightmare on Elm Street* series so we can have a horror movie marathon. It's so much fun watching scary movies with them because they freak out and jump and scream, usually they end up each hugging onto a side of me.

Lately, though, it's been a little different being around the two of them. I've been noticing girls more and more. Their assets—eyes, legs, butts, and of course, you can't forget their boobs. My dad picked up on it and gave me 'The Talk' which was really embarrassing and yet, sort of interesting. He asked if I was having any feelings toward Jessica or Katherine. I told him no because I don't want them changing our rules about sleepovers and stuff. I really don't have those feelings for Jessica; she's really pretty but she's just my friend. Katherine, though, she's amazing. I love her eyes and she's so pretty *and* she's my best friend. Every time I see her I want to hug her *and* kiss her. I have to keep telling myself we're just friends because I don't even know if she likes me like that. There are a few girls at school that really seem to like me but they just aren't her.

I've started hanging out with some guys from my baseball team, too. I don't see Jessica and Katherine as much as before, but we're all okay with it. I don't want to sit around and talk about NSYNC while they paint their nails and do their hair. One of the guys on my team has a twin sister, Riley, and she likes me *a lot*. We've been talking on the phone every night, and she keeps hinting she wants me to be her boyfriend, but it just doesn't feel right. I talked to Jessica about her and she thinks I should go for it. I talk to Jessica about most stuff, including girls, but part of me feels like if I talk to Katherine about girls it will hurt our friendship. I don't think Jessica ever tells her what we talk about. We're the Three Musketeers, but we have our own relationships, too.

Pulling myself from my thoughts, I jump on my bike and ride over to Katherine's house. She's going to be so excited! We got her and Jessica front row tickets with meet and greet passes for NSYNC this summer for her birthday. My dad used to go to school with someone at their label and was able to pull some strings. After putting my bike in the garage, I walk into the house. None of us ever knock we all just kind of share houses and parents. Except for Joseph, he keeps his distance. Today he's in Paris so Maryanne is running the show as usual. I feel bad for Katherine, she's lucky if Joseph remembers her birthday. Maryanne took Katherine and Jessica to the pier this morning to keep up Lila's tradition so I'm sure she's a little sad.

I walk upstairs but pause on the landing when I hear my name. I'm outside in the hall so they can't see me.

"Katherine, you have to tell Michael. You're being dumb. I'm sure he would want to know."

Katherine exhales loudly, "Drop it, Jessica. We don't talk about these kinds of things. If it's meant to happen it will."

"You're so stupid sometimes. What are you going to do if he starts dating someone? What then?"

"Jessica, we're both going to date people, it's what happens. Do you really think you can date someone when you're thirteen and end up with them forever? He's my best friend and it's going to stay that way."

"Whatever, Katie Grace, I think it's dumb. You guys are perfect for each other and neither of you realize it." Jessica only calls her Katie Grace when she's emotional. I wish I would have heard the beginning of their talk. Listening to them talk about Katherine dating someone else makes my stomach drop.

I guess it's safe to go in now that they're done talking. "Happy Birthday!" I spin her in a circle and she laughs. God, she always smells so good.

"Thank you! What took you so long to get here?"

I smirk at her. "I was putting together the best present in the history of all presents ever given, and it took a little longer than I thought it would." She reaches out her hands in a 'give me' motion. I laugh and shake my head. "Nope, this one is so good that you're going to open it in front of everyone."

I really want to make sure Marc sees her open the best gift. He's a jerk and he wants to date Katherine. I heard him telling his friends one day that she would be his eventually. *That's not going to happen if I can help it.* I hate Marc.

Katherine gives me her best puppy dog eyes. *"Please, Michael.* I'll tell everyone what you gave me, but I want to open it now." I just shake my head at her and laugh. *She's so adorable.*

"Fine, be that way then." She's so funny when she tries to act mad. I grab her around the waist and tickle her. "Stop pouting, I promise it will be worth the wait."

"Come on, let's go help Maryanne, you two. I swear, sometimes you guys don't act like just friends." Katherine stills and I let her go. We follow Jessica downstairs just as Maryanne lets Marc in the door. Suddenly, I can't wait for the party to be over.

There are lots of people here and I haven't talked to Katherine much because Marc has been hanging on her all night. When he's around, I typically keep my distance. She comes up beside me and bumps into my shoulder. "Stop it, Michael."

When I turn to her, I can't miss the sadness on her face. "Stop what?" She gives me that 'you know what I mean' look.

"Stop avoiding me because of Marc. He's my *friend,* Michael, and I'm not going to ignore him because you don't like him. It's *my* day and I want you to talk to me, too. *Please.*" *I hate when she looks at me like that, with her big green eyes, because they make me want to do anything she wants.* Since it's her birthday, I really should be making more of an effort to be nice.

"Okay, I'll be nice. What do you want to do now?"

Her smile is huge as she pulls me by the hand and drags me across the yard. Her enthusiasm is contagious. "It's time to open presents and I want to open yours first."

I laugh; she can never wait for surprises. "No. You need to open mine last. It's important to me, okay?"

She peers up at me with those big green eyes again, suddenly solemn. "Okay, but you have to sit next to me while I open them."

"Deal."

Katherine opened a ton of gifts. Marc got them both annual passes to Disneyland. *Great, now they can spend even more time together.* Of course she loved it; she *loves* Disneyland. She gave him a quick hug and went back to opening her gifts. I don't like how her hugging him makes me feel. AT ALL. Their relationship makes me so mad. I know one of these days I'm going to knock him out, and I can't wait for that day to come. When she finally opens my gift her reaction is awesome. "Oh my god! Jessica, oh my god! Michael, are these for real? Like really, *really* real?" I nod my head at her as a huge smile spreads across my face. Katherine screams the loudest scream I think I've ever heard and does a happy dance. When she's done with her happy dance, she wraps me up in the biggest hug and kisses me on the cheek.

"You are seriously *the best*! God, I freaking love you! Jessica LOOK! Michael and his parents got us NSYNC tickets with meet and greets! OH MY GOD!" Suddenly, all of the girls are screaming, not just Jessica and Katherine. I love that my present made her so happy. I love it even more that Marc's smug look is gone from his face. I don't know why he thinks just because his mom died, too, that he has special rights to her. They became close friends by bonding over their losses. Their 'soul keepers' crap makes me want to puke. *I* was the one that got Katherine back from the edge, not him. He has no idea what it was like, what *she* was like.

Katherine went inside to thank my parents for the tickets while I talked to Jessica. Thank god Marc stayed away. "That was an amazing present, Michael. *Really* cool. Can I ask you something?"

"Sure, Jessica, you know you can ask me anything." Jessica looks around to make sure no one is listening. "Riley is a *huge* NSYNC fan. Why didn't you give those tickets to her and go with her?"

I'm confused. "Why would I do that? You guys love them, too, *and* you're my best friends. Riley is just some girl."

She raises an eyebrow at me. "Come on. Michael, *you know* Riley wants to be your girlfriend. She's telling everyone you're going to be her first boyfriend *and* her first kiss."

I kick my feet a little bit and my stomach feels sick. "Maybe that's what she wants and maybe I want that, too, I don't know. But I know that those tickets were meant for you guys, *not* Riley."

"Whatever, Michael. Your actions speak louder than words. You obviously like Katherine more than Riley. You need to sort your feelings out. You can't sit here and be mad at Marc all night because he wants to be her boyfriend if you don't."

Now it's my turn to look around and make sure no one is listening. "Jessica, if I did want to date her, and I'm not saying I do, but if I did, would you be mad or sad about it?"

Jessica laughs at me loudly. "Um, no, dude, not at all. We're friends and we'll always be best friends no matter what. You're going to be my boyfriend butt kicking, ninja fighting protector 'til the end, but we're *always* just going to be friends. You and Katie Grace…Well, you two are different, you've always been linked. I've been waiting for what seems like forever for you two to finally admit your feelings for each other. Now that we're all old enough for boyfriends and girlfriends, it's time."

So this is what they were talking about earlier. I figured, but now I definitely know for sure. She says it like it's just an inevitable fact, but I'm not so sure. "I don't know, Jessica, I don't want to mess anything up but I'll think about it, okay?"

"Yeah, okay, but you should know that Marc has a game of spin the bottle all lined up and he's hoping to land on Katherine." *He's such a dick, I'm not going to let him do that to her.*

"Jessica, you have to play first and get the bottle to land on Marc."

She looks at me like I'm crazy. "Eww, Michael no, that's *not* going to happen."

"Come on, Jessica, you already had your first kiss and Katherine hasn't. That first kiss is supposed to be *ours* not hers and Marc's!"

"Ha! I knew it! You *do* like her! Fine, I'll get it to land on Marc but you *better* get it to land on Katherine."

Relief pours through me. "Done. Let's go. I don't see him anywhere."

"Yeah, the parents went to eat down by the pool so everyone was heading back in the house. Let's go."

When we get upstairs, there's a group of about four kids who want to play spin the bottle. Marc is one of them but Katherine is standing back. *I don't think she wants to play ...thank God.*

"What's going on up here?" Gotta love Jessica, she gets right to the point.

Marc answers her immediately, "Spin the bottle, you in?"

Jessica turns in a circle to see how many people are playing. "Just the four of you are playing? That seems kind of lame."

"No, not just the four of us, Katherine is playing, aren't you Katherine?" She nods her head yes but doesn't actually say the words.

Jessica nods her head at Marc, "Then I'm in, too. You in, Michael?"

I guess it's now or never. "Yeah sure, why not?"

Marc set the bottle on the floor and one girl backs out at the last second, which is good, now we're evenly numbered. "Ladies first. Who wants to spin?"

There are only three of them, but this girl, Jill, from Katherine's gymnastic team volunteers. When Jill spins the bottle, I watch it closely to see how hard and fast it spins, trying to calculate my best chance of making it land on Katherine. The bottle lands on –Dean—he looks really happy and so does Jill. He takes her hand and leads her out to somewhere with more privacy I guess.

Jessica jumps up and spins it next, winking at me while Marc keeps his line of sight on Katherine. I'm not sure how she did it, but she got it to land on Marc. I'll give it to him; he doesn't look all that disappointed to be kissing Jessica. "Come on, Marc, let's go find some privacy." Jessica pulls him from the room and I'm flooded with relief.

"Your turn, Katherine. Do you want to spin or do you want to quit? You don't have to kiss me if you don't want to." I inch closer to her with every word that I speak. I've never wanted to kiss her as much as I do right now.

She looks up at me shyly. "I want to play, but I guess there's no need to spin since it's just the two of us."

No, there really isn't.

"Katherine, I need to say something first." I lead her to the bed, sitting on the edge, placing my forehead against hers.

"Okay."

"I just wanted to tell you that I'm not doing this just because of the game. I've wanted to kiss you for a while, but you're my best friend and I don't want to wreck that. When Jessica told me Marc was playing so he could kiss you, I knew I couldn't let that happen. No matter what else happens, our first kiss should be with each other, right?"

I've got one hand on each side of her face now, our foreheads still together, and we're so close. I just need to hear her say it, and when she does, it's just a whisper, "Right."

I lean in, placing my lips on hers. They're so warm and she tastes like bubblegum lip gloss. I have no clue what I'm doing, but my body is acting on its own. I move my lips against hers and she kisses me back. It's just a simple, perfect kiss. I pull back and look into her eyes, they're sparking with happiness.

Neither of us speaks, but the need to kiss her again is overwhelming. I move forward, my lips brushing against hers. This time I open my mouth a little and so does she. Our tongues touch briefly, but it's long enough for me to know I love kissing her and don't want to kiss anyone else. We slowly break apart.

"Happy Birthday, Katherine."

She looks up at me shyly. "Thank you, Michael, I think that was my favorite part of the day."

I smile at her and take her hand. "Come on, let's go find everyone else."

~~~***~~~

Later that night, long after the party was over, and after we'd watched two *Nightmare on Elm Street* movies, we rolled out our sleeping bags on Katherine's floor. Jessica had crashed on the bed during the movie so we left her there. I love the nights we get to sleep over because we don't have to use our walkie talkies to talk.

"So, are we okay now?" *Well, that was random.*

I turn over in my sleeping bag and face her. "Why wouldn't we be?"

She sighs, "Because we kissed and I just want to know we're still going to be friends now because kissing can change things."

"I know it can, but we don't have to let it, do we? I *wanted* to kiss you, Katherine. Do you regret it?"

"No! I could never regret that. But, we don't talk about this kind of stuff and I know Riley really likes you."

I really don't *ever* want to talk to her about other girls. "I know she does"

"And you like her, too."

This sucks. "I do, but I don't have to anymore, not now, but do you like Marc?"

She's quiet for a while. "No, I don't, not like that. I'm glad Jessica landed on him. But…." She sounds sad. I wish I could see her face better but it's dark.

"But what?"

"It's just that I like *you* like that, and I don't want to. I don't want you to like Riley or anything but I think you should. We're best friends always and forever, Michael. But don't you see the kids in our class that try dating and then a week after they kiss it gets all weird they don't even *like* each other anymore? I just don't want that for us. I think we need to wait if we want to, you know… be a couple."

This is so hard to talk about. I'm glad she doesn't like Marc like that, but she's right, too. Everyone *does* break up after kissing. Our kiss was special and I don't want to mess that up. "So we'll wait then and see what happens. We don't have to be boyfriend and girlfriend, but I'm glad our first kiss was with each other."

"Me, too. Goodnight, Michael."

"Goodnight, Katherine."

Chapter 4 ~ Catch Me, I'm Falling

"Eeekk! I'm so excited! Are you really going to do it tonight, Michael? I'll totally just tell Katherine I have cramps so you two can go alone."

She's too –much—sometimes I really wish my other best friend was a guy. "TMI, Jessica, keep that shit to yourself. I don't want to know about your cramps, but yes, tonight."

I've decided that since we're starting high school on Monday, I want to make it official and ask Katherine to be my girlfriend. I've dated off and on since our kiss but she hasn't. No kisses. No boyfriends. She *did* go out on maybe two movie dates but that's it. I dated Riley after the party, and we did a lot of making out, but it never came close to the feeling I got when I kissed Katherine. It never did with anyone. I'm tired of waiting. I know I want Katherine, and from Jessica's reaction, I'm pretty sure she wants me, too.

"Michael, it's going to be so romantic. Are your parents still planning on staying on Joseph's boat?"

"Yeah, they are. His boat is much bigger than ours and they have business associates staying over. The only reason they said we could stay on our boat alone is because the Captain is there getting it ready to take out for the holiday next week." I hear her sigh on the other end of the phone. "What's up, Jessica?"

"I'm just really happy for you guys. My best friends are *finally* going to be together, and that's great, but I just hope our friendship doesn't change."

Oh, I can see why she might feel like that. "Don't worry, Jessica, it's always going to be the three of us just like before. I don't think things will change much, but if they do, tell me and we'll fix it. You're out so much now with the kids from your singing club that we're without you more often than not already."

"Very true, Matthews, and since summer is over I'll only get to see them on the weekends anyway. So tell me, are you worried about Marc?"

"Fuck no. I'm not worried about that douchebag. I swear, Jessica, I don't get what she sees in his friendship. All I ever see is him wanting to get in her pants."

She's laughing and it strikes a nerve. "It's not funny!" That makes her laugh even harder.

"I'm sorry, Michael, but it totally is. First of all, Katherine doesn't see him that way, trust me. You're the only one she thinks of like that. And secondly, watch your language. If your dad hears you he'll be pissed you broke the 'no cussing until I'm an adult' rule that he stuck you with after you beat Bryce's ass."

All of a sudden, I'm the one laughing. That was the only thing he'd said about that whole thing. 'No cussing until you're eighteen, buddy, and if I hear that you do there will be hell to pay.' "I know, but fuck, I hate him. He needs to leave Katherine alone."

"You know, for what it's worth, you should try to figure out a way to get past that. They have a different kind of friendship. They talk about each other's love interests and stuff like we do. They're close like we are but almost closer because of the whole mom thing. It's not a battle you'll win, Michael, and I don't think you should try. Just talk to me when you're mad about him. I know you don't think it's the same because I definitely *don't* want to get in your pants. But it is because *she* doesn't want to get into his. She cherishes you and that's why she blew him off tonight to watch the meteor shower with *you*. You know that stars are *their* thing. So calm down, pick your battles, and go get your girl."

I feel so much better after talking to Jessica, but I'm still so nervous that I just threw up. I've always hated that about myself—my emotions make me puke. So, after my second shower of the day, I'm finally ready to go.

"Are you ready, Michael? Tonight's the big night, right?"

My dad couldn't be happier that I'm finally asking Katherine to be my girlfriend. He and my mom have been hoping for this since we were kids. "It is, but it's not that big of a deal, so please don't make it into one. I'm just asking her to be my girlfriend... we're not getting married."

He pats me on the shoulder. "It *is* a big deal. The two of you have been attached at the hip since you were seven years old. This is a big step, Michael. You guys are growing up, and after tonight, things will be different. Also, don't forget...after tonight, if she says yes, no more sleepovers. I'm happy for you, kiddo. I know how long you've waited to finally make this happen."

"Thanks, Dad, but let's get her to say yes first. The sleepover rule is dumb. What difference does it make if we're dating? If we wanted to do it, not having a sleepover wouldn't stop us."

He smiles at me, "Maybe not, but it makes your mother feel better, so that's what's going to happen. You're lucky she agreed to one last sleepover tonight. Come on, let's go get your girl."

~~~***~~~

"Michael, this is going to be so much fun! Too bad Jessica wasn't feeling well. I can't wait for the shower to start!" We've been on the boat for a few hours and the meteor shower is supposed to start soon. Katherine is sitting next to me on the chaise lounge out on the deck. I'm nervous and am having a hard time thinking of things to say without blurting out what I want to ask her, especially since she's sitting so close to me. The scent of her gardenia perfume lingers between us; it's my favorite scent in the world.

"How was the movie you and Marc went to earlier?"

A funny look flashes across her face and she's hesitant to answer, "It was okay."

"Just okay? I thought you were looking forward to it."

Again with that look. *What the hell?*

"I was, but can we just drop it please? This isn't something we usually talk about and I don't want to make you mad."

"Why would I be mad?"

She avoids my gaze, instead looking up at the stars. "Look, Michael, it's starting!"

I pull her in close and wrap my arm around her shoulder. It's nothing new but it feels like more and yet, it's *still* not enough. I need to feel her if we're about to have the conversation I think we're going to. Leaning my head against hers, I push the subject. We *need* to talk about this.

"Katherine, you're avoiding the question."

She sighs, "Can't we just watch and talk later? I don't want to fight with you over nothing."

"If it was nothing you wouldn't have an issue talking about it and there wouldn't be anything to fight over." My temper is flaring, and I've got a sinking feeling in my stomach that he asked her to be his girlfriend.

"Fine, Michael! He kissed me! Is that what you want to hear? Do you feel better now knowing that? We don't do this. We don't talk about things like this, it's too hard!"

He kissed her. Fuck me. I've never hated someone as much as I hate him in this moment.

"Did you kiss him back?"

She won't look at me. *Damn.* "Katherine, did you kiss him back?"

Finally, she looks at me with tears in her eyes. "Yes, at first, but then I stopped."

Interesting... "Why did you stop?"

Her voice is barely a whisper, "Because it wasn't the same, it didn't feel the same"

Yes! This is my chance. "The same as what, Katherine?" *Oh, maybe that was the wrong thing to say. She looks pissed now.*

"Are you really going to make me say it, Michael?"

I need to hear her say it. "Yes"

She squeezes her eyes shut before she speaks, "It wasn't the same as you, okay? With you, it was special, and with Marc, it was just a boy kissing me."

Hell yes. It's now or never.

"I know it's not, it's never the same. No one else has been the same since I kissed you, either. I don't think anyone else ever will be. I want you, Katie Grace, and only you. Will you be my girlfriend?"

Her big green eyes are filled with tears, but she's nodding her head yes. "It's only you, Michael. It's always been that way. I feel bad for Marc but I just don't like him like that."

I place my hand on the back of her neck and pull her in so I can finally kiss her. "Don't feel bad about him; he knows it's supposed to be us. I love you, Katherine."

"I love you too, Michael."

Our lips meet so softly and already the feeling is back. I don't care if I'm too young to know what I want. I know that her lips were made for mine. I increase the pace of the kiss and she opens her mouth to mine. Our tongues meet, and she's hesitant at first, but I pull her in closer and guide her. This is by far the most amazing kiss I've ever had. Pulling back, I rest my head against hers.

"Wow," she giggles at me, "That was definitely wow. Thank you, Michael."

Um, okay, I'm confused. "Thanks for…?"

"Waiting for me, being there for me, catching me when I fall."

I pull her in between my legs and she leans against me, looking up at the sky.

"Always, Katherine, it was never an option. Being without you isn't an option. Letting you fall isn't an option. Everything that's happened from the day we met until now has built up to this, to us. And now that we're together, tell Marc hands *and* lips off from now on."

She laces her hands into mine. "That's not a problem, I pretty much told him that today. You better tell Riley the same thing."

"Already done, but there's something you should know. My parents, really my mom, said we can't have any more sleepovers."

She bursts into laughter, "Oh my god, I can't believe you had that conversation with your parents. As if we would do that! We just kissed for the first time in almost two years! I don't plan on anything more for a long time. They have *nothing* to worry about."

"I know they don't, but tonight it's just the two of us and we have two years of making out to catch up on. I think it might take us all night."

"I think you're right. We need to make up for lost time while we have the chance."

Chapter 5 ~ We Fall Together

"Okay, Michael, you guys are all set for tonight. Joseph and your parents landed in Paris about a half hour ago. They already checked in with Maryanne and she knows she's on call if Katherine needs anything or wants to come over. We're going for mani-pedis in an hour, and after that she's yours for the night. I can't believe you two are finally going to have sex! Your days of whacking it in the shower are over."

I accidentally spilled my shower habit to Jessica one night when I was drunk at a party. I don't care that she knows; I know she would never tell. We have our own personal secrets from Katherine just like they have theirs from me. I can talk to Jessica the way most guys talk to their guy friends. It works for us. I couldn't imagine it any other way.

"Well, thanks for that. Damn, Jessica, one drunken slip up and you hold it over me forever. Besides, you should be happy I'm taking care of business in the shower instead of cheating on your friend like other guys do."

"Yeah, like *that* would ever happen. You love her just as much, if not more, than I do. I think that it's great you guys didn't rush this. I wish I would've waited to find someone that lasted longer than six months. I'm happy for you both. This is huge! Besides, you're the only guy I can talk to about stuff like this and not only get the truth, but also a *guy's* truth."

"Always. Never doubt that you can talk to me about anything. I gotta go finish getting ready, but text me when you get to the nail place so I can go set up."

Tonight is the night. I've already done my emotional puking so I'm all good there…I hope. I've got candles, roses, and dinner ordered…I just need to pick it up. I want everything to be perfect for her. We've waited so long for this night. It's not a surprise; we planned everything together, talked about birth control, and made sure it's what we both really want. As much as I'm dying to have sex, I'll wait as long as it takes for her to be ready.

~~~***~~~

Jessica texted me that Katherine had just dropped her off and she should be arriving soon. Dinner is waiting on the candlelit table, and I even popped open a bottle of champagne. I don't want to get her drunk, just help take the edge off for both of us. Upstairs, there are flowers and candles waiting, along with the present I got her.

"Michael, are you here?"

I was so lost in thought I didn't even hear her come in. "I'm right here, babe. How was your day?"

Her smile lights up my soul from the inside. She looks beautiful. "My day was good, but it's better now that you're here. It looks and smells amazing in here. I can't believe you did all of this."

I pull her close and inhale her gardenia perfume. She smells incredible; it's still my favorite scent in the world. I whisper to her as I kiss a path to her mouth, "There's nothing I wouldn't do for you, just ask and anything you want is yours."

She trembles slightly, but in a good way, and whispers back so softly, "Okay."

My mouth finds hers and she opens to me without hesitation, pulling me into a very passionate kiss. I'm the first to break away, even though all I want to do is take her upstairs and make love to her.

"Come on, let's eat." I pull out her chair and give her a quick kiss on the cheek. We're both obviously nervous and dinner is mostly quiet.

"The champagne is good, are you trying to get me drunk?"

I choke a little on my spaghetti but see the twinkle in her eyes and know she's teasing. "Never. I don't want either of us to be drunk the first time we have sex. I want to experience this *with* you. I just thought the champagne would relax us a little. Do you still want to do this? We can wait, babe, there's no rush if you're not ready."

She glances up at me shyly, "I'm ready. I'm nervous, but I'm beyond ready to make love to you. It's me and you always, from beginning to end, right?"

I take her hand and pull her up. "Me and you, always. Come on, I have a gift waiting for you upstairs."

She giggles "Yeah, I know you do"

"Katherine Grace Moore! I have an actual present for you. But, I won't argue if you want to tell me I'm God's gift to women *after* I make love to you."

She slaps my shoulder as we reach her room. "Yeah, Matthews, not gonna happen, but I *can* already tell you that you're God's gift to me."

I think she definitely has that mixed up. If she wasn't in my life I would be lost.

I watch her facial expressions as she takes in the room. There are two dozen roses in a vase on her dresser and I'd hung white twinkly lights from the ceiling and lit a few candles to help set the mood. I thought maybe the twinkly lights would remind her of our night under the stars when I asked her to be my girlfriend.

"Michael, it's beautiful. Thank you for making this so special."

I lead her to the bed and hand her the small box that holds the bracelet I got her. I thought about the gift for a while and was pretty sure I'd come up with the perfect one. It's a platinum charm bracelet with an engravable plate. The inscription says 'Fall into me' and the only charm on it is a catcher's glove. Since I'm a catcher in baseball, and hers in life, I thought it was perfect.

Her hands tremble with excitement as she opens the box. Tears flow freely from her eyes as she takes it in. *That's my girl; she's always crying for the good and the bad.* "It's beautiful, absolutely perfect. I couldn't imagine a better gift. I'm never going to take it off. Can you put it on me please?"

My IPod has been playing softly in the background this entire time with a bunch of slow songs. As I latched the bracelet on her wrist, Boyz II Men's *I'll Make Love to You* begins to play.

I pull her into an embrace and kiss her tenderly, allowing all of my emotions and love to flow through me and into this kiss. She pulls me in even closer, gripping my hair in her hands, moaning into my mouth, and I know she feels it, too.

I stepped back, needing more—needing to hear her say the words. "Katherine, can I make love to you?"

The look on her face is filled with love. "Yes, Michael, please make love to me."

She's so beautiful. She's wearing an emerald green sundress that matches her eyes. Her gorgeous auburn curls fall perfectly down her back. The best part is the look of desire in her eyes. She wants *me*, and it's an absolutely erotic feeling. I begin kissing her again, slowly, taking my time as I guide my hand slowly up her thigh. We've messed around before, so my hands know exactly where to go and how to please her, but I want to see her; I've never seen all of her before. My pants grow tighter just thinking about it. Taking her hand in mine, I help her up and slowly peel off her dress. *She's breathtaking.* Her soft curves are beautiful, her skin glowing in the candlelight. The pink lace panties and bra she's wearing exquisitely cover all she's about to give me. *She's mine, she's giving herself to me and it's the greatest gift I have ever received.* A blush creeps up her face but she remains standing, eyes hooded with desire, letting me take her and this moment in completely. *If I don't get my jeans off now they're going to bust open all on their own, I'm so ready for her.*

I don't break eye contact with her; I couldn't even if I wanted to. I want this vision of her imprinted in my mind for eternity. I don't ever want to forget how she looks in this moment. I begin to undress, first taking off my shirt. She's told me many times her favorite thing to see is me without my shirt on. As her gaze flitters across my upper body, I pull my pants off, finally feeling slight relief. Her eyes grow bigger as she takes in my hard on under my boxer briefs. I lace my fingers in hers and lower us both to the bed.

My hands graze along her curvy thighs and across her stomach up to her beautiful breasts. I love the sounds that she makes as she absorbs all the pleasure. I want to be sure she feels how much I love her through my actions as I continue to explore her body with my hands and mouth. Her whimpers of pleasure are pushing me to continue. I gently slip off her panties and unclasp her bra. Before I remove my boxers, I want to make sure she's absolutely ready for this. "Are you sure, baby? We can stop, just say the word."

"Make love to me, Michael."

That's all I need to hear. I remove my boxers and lower myself between her legs. I'm trying so hard to be gentle. I don't want to hurt her any more than I know it's already going to. Although I'm taking it painstakingly slow, she still cries out in pain. Clenching her even closer to me, I kiss her deeply. Before I get a chance to pull out and save her even more pain, she pulls me in slowly until we're fully connected. The feeling of being inside her is indescribable. I'm connected to her in a way I don't want to be with anyone else. Ever. *I'm so in love with this girl.* I make a vow to myself to never be anything *but* tender with her.

After it's over, we lay in each other's arms for hours, talking. Her arms are my favorite place to be. Eventually, though, we get up, change the sheets, and take separate showers. While the water falls down on me, I actually shed a few tears. I don't know why—maybe it's happiness or relief that she's completely mine after years of love and friendship. I just know that nothing will ever take her away from me. *I will love this girl until the day I die.*

Chapter 6 ~ The Big Day

"Hey, kiddo, I just wanted to check in on things and see if you need anything for tonight before I go to work." My dad walks over to my nightstand and picks up the ring box, looking inside. "For what it's worth, I think she's going to love it and I can't imagine her saying *anything* but yes. It's hard to believe you two are heading off to college and getting engaged. You are both very blessed to be best friends and in love. I'm so proud of you both."

I wipe the sleep from my eyes and sit up in bed. Looking at the clock, it's only six a.m. "Thanks, Dad. I think I have everything, I'm just nervous."

He takes a seat on the edge of my bed. "Michael, it's natural to be nervous, but no one knows when the time is right but you. You've been hanging on to that ring for over a year and I fully agree that proposing in high school would have been the wrong idea. You're heading off to college now; it seems like a natural progression to me. Have a long engagement, or hell, marry that girl tomorrow. She worships you and I know you worship her, too. I never imagined my son wouldn't play the field before settling down, but seeing lots of women isn't always all it's cracked up to be, either."

I shake my head at him, "Not the conversation I want to be having at six in the morning. But I don't need to play the field to know that she's the love of my life and that will never change."

He ruffles my hair as if I'm a little kid again. "Okay, I get it. Tell me the plan again for this weekend."

"Jessica packed her bag and we took it to the boat yesterday so Katherine will have clothes for the weekend. We're spending the day at the beach, and after I propose I'm taking her straight to the boat. The captain is going to take us out for two uninterrupted days of fun."

My dad clears his throat, "Well, just because you're going to be getting married doesn't mean you don't need to be safe."

I cut him off, "Dad, stop, please. We've had the sex talk many times. I'm not going to knock her up."

He gets off the bed, "Alright, I know you've got it handled. Text me tonight when you get to the boat. Love you, son."

"Love you, too, Dad, I will."

I know he worries and probably rightfully so. He knows I wish I wasn't going to college. What he doesn't know is that I wish that Katherine and I were starting our family already instead of having to wait God knows how many more years to get to that point. Sometimes I wonder what's wrong with me. Instead of thinking about getting pussy, I'm wishing for babies. Our friends seem to understand how in love we are and no one has ever really tried to come between us all these years. Riley has always given me subtle hints that she's available as soon as we crash and burn and God only knows what Marc has planned for Katherine. Truth be told, I don't even want another girl. As soon as I think about anyone else even *touching* Katherine, my temper flares to a scary level of rage. The sound of my phone ringing pulls me from my thoughts.

"Hey, Jessica. A little early, isn't it?"

She laughs, "Yeah no, I'm on my way up the stairs so cover your ass up."

Why is she here so early? So much for going back to sleep.

I lean up against the headboard and cover myself with my blanket just as she breezes through the door. "Why are you still in bed? Today is the biggest day of your life so far; don't you have tons of stuff to do?" She hands me a coffee, which I take gratefully, and then she grabs the ring box and plops down on my bed.

"You *are* dressed, right?"

I smirk at her. "Yup, in my boxers." She scoots to the other side of the bed.

"What, you can't be next to me?"

She looks me up and down. "I can be next to you just fine. It's your morning wood I want to be a few feet away from."

I laugh so hard I choke on my coffee. "You don't need to worry about that, my morning wood is long gone. I don't know why you're here so early. I don't have anything to do except pack the picnic. We took everything to the boat last night and I have nine hours before I'm meeting Katherine."

She sighs deeply, "Whatever, Michael, I'm freaking out! My best friends are getting engaged, you're getting freaking married! I'm nervous for you, I'm excited for you, and I'm seriously in love with this ring. She's going to love it. Why aren't *you* a freaking wreck right now? If it were me, I'd be a ball of nerves. Hell, it isn't me and I'm *still* a ball of nerves."

Even first thing in the morning she's high strung. "How much coffee have you had?"

She gives me the evil eye. "None. I don't need coffee, I've got a chai tea. I was being *nice* and brought coffee for *you* because I thought you would have had a sleepless night. But I guess I was wrong because you look very well rested."

"Jessica, I have loved Katherine for as long as I can remember. The only thing that makes me excessively nervous is how nervous *you* are. Yes, I have some nerves, that makes me human. But I don't see her turning me down, do you? Is there something I should know?"

"Oh god, no! I'm sorry if I gave you that impression. She loves you and you two are going to be so happy. You're going to have beautiful babies with blonde hair and emerald green eyes and I'm going to be the best auntie/godmother around. I'm just excited for you both and thought I would come over and spend the day with you. It's probably going to be one of the last ones we really get to spend together for a while."

She's so sensitive; I should've known this was going to affect her. "Jessica, I would love to spend the day with you. We're all best friends. I know things are going to change, but I don't think they're going to change as much as you think. But if you start feeling alone or left out, speak up. I don't want to hurt you, regardless of my marrying Katherine. You're always going to be my best friend. If it weren't for you running interference between us all these years, we wouldn't even be here. You know we don't have the best track record when it comes to talking out our feelings to each other. I wish we did because maybe then she wouldn't need Marc so much. I'm hoping now we'll close that gap in our relationship.

She pats my hand, trying to reassure me. "Look, you've dealt with Marc for years. I know you'll never be friends, but maybe you should start considering him an ally instead of an enemy. Regardless of how you feel about him, he *always* encourages her to follow her heart."

"Oh, come on! He's just waiting until the time is right and then he's going to take advantage of her."

"Really? Can you step out of the 1950's for a minute and at least give her credit for being able to make her own decisions? Katherine is one of the strongest people I know. If Marc ever gets the chance to 'take advantage of her' I can guarantee you it would only happen if she was a willing participant. Honestly. Michael, you've got to get over this. Let it go. Stop trying to dominate her relationships. She's about to be your wife for Christ's sake. She would never, *ever* cheat on you.

Now, we're *way* off topic. Tell me what you have planned today, down to every last detail."

I'm slowly nursing my coffee as I listen to Jessica rant at me. *Maybe I am too overprotective, but I can't help it. I've been that way since we were kids and I'm not stopping anytime soon.* "Let's just agree to disagree about Marc, okay? I hear what you're saying, but my opinion of him will *never* change. Katherine is coming here to pick me up after her lunch with my dad. After that, we're heading to the beach for some down time where we'll have a picnic dinner and watch the sunset. I figure at some point while we're stargazing I'll pop the question. When she says yes we'll head to the boat. I've got my IPod set up and all her favorite songs loaded. I'm sure we'll do some dancing under the stars before I take her to my room where I plan to keep her for two days."

Nodding, she replies, "Did you load that sappy sad song that she loves?" She's talking about *When She Danced,* the theme song from the movie *Stealing Home*."Absolutely. We've watched my parents dance to that song so many times. Katherine's always been so in love with it and with the amount of love my parents have for each other. I knew that song should be first on the playlist."

"Sounds like you have it all under control. So hit me with the proposal."

I shoot her a dirty look, "No."

"What do you mean no? You practiced it, right?"

"Yes."

"Then let me hear it."

"Jessica, it's private."

She isn't going to take no for an answer, "Michael, you need a female opinion on this. You know how Katherine cries at everything. You want her happy tears tonight. Let's make sure she gets them."

I hate it when she's right. I know if Jessica loves it, Katherine will, too.

I reluctantly give in, because even if I think it's perfect, this is something I don't want to screw up. "Fine."

After taking a deep breath, I recite the proposal I've been working on for what seems like years.

"Katherine, when I was seven years old and my dad brought me to meet you for the first time, I never would have imagined that moment changing my life forever. From that first day, we had an unbreakable connection, and although I didn't know what it was back then, I knew that I liked it. Over the years, that connection has grown stronger, *we've* grown stronger, and our *love* has grown stronger. There's not a doubt in my mind that I was brought here for you and only you. I know I can be overprotective and demanding but it's part of how I show my love. You're my everything, forever and always, mine to catch when you fall, mine to love and cherish until the day I die. There's never been anyone else and there never will be. You're *it* for me, Katherine.

You're the keeper of my heart until the end of time. Marry me, love me, and only me, have babies with me, spend your life with me, and I promise I'll spend my entire life worshipping every single bit of your love. Katherine Grace Moore, will you please do me the absolute honor of becoming my wife?"

I look up at Jessica just as she punches me in the shoulder. "You fucker, you made me cry and mess up my makeup. That was…there are no words. Michael, that was the most perfect proposal I've ever heard. I should have never doubted you for a minute. You guys got this. You and Katie Grace are going to have the happily ever after we all dream of."

Chapter 7 ~ Freefalling

It's been an entire day since my dad died and every second that has passed has felt like an eternity. I keep hoping I'll wake up from this nightmare and everything will be okay. Yet, deep down inside, I know that this is my new normal. I have to get up and at least piece myself together enough to go make funeral arrangements. Since my last argument with my mom, we haven't spoken. But I *did* tell her I would take care of it because I know she can't. The doctor sedated her yesterday after our fight—that was probably a good thing. She was being such a rapacious bitch.

I've got the housekeeper running interference on the phone and the door. I swear, people don't have any decency. *You want to pay your condolences, fine, but do it after the funeral and give us time to grieve.* Between the food and the flowers, the whole fucking house smells like a cross between a florist and a buffet. I get it, people are sorry and they want to help, but they can help more by leaving me the fuck alone.

I glance over at my phone on the charger, knowing I can't ignore it forever and finally pick it up. Between Jessica and Katherine, both my text messages *and* voicemails are at capacity. I draw in the deepest breath I can and begin listening to and reading them all. It takes me an hour to get through them but I can't respond. I don't even know what to say, or if I want to say anything at all.

I turn the shower on high and let the water wash over me, hoping for relief that never comes.

My hands begin to tremble and my body starts shaking. Before I realize what's happening, I'm down on the tile floor, crying harder than I ever have in my life. I'm filled with so much rage and have no clue where or who to direct it at. What I do know is that I really need a fucking drink.

Eventually, I get out, go through the motions of getting ready, and head out to the funeral home. When I walk outside, Jessica is propped against her car at the curb. I can tell she's upset and I just don't have it in me to deal with her at the moment.

"Leave, Jessica, I'm not in the mood."

She flinches so hard it's as if I'd hit her, but she doesn't leave. "Where are you going?"

"Out."

"Stop it, Michael. Talk to me. I want to help you. Out where?"

I pause for a minute, taking a deep breath and willing myself to say the words out loud. "To the funeral home, to make... the arrangements."

Nodding, she answers, "I'm coming with you."

"No."

She laughs a crazy fucking laugh and I wonder if I'm not the only one losing my shit. "You don't get a say in this, Matthews. You're my best friend and you're not doing this alone. I'M COMING WITH YOU AND THAT'S FINAL. We're taking my car, too. You're in no condition to drive."

I can't really argue with that, but as I close the door, I need to make one thing perfectly fucking clear to her. "Jessica, don't talk to me about her, not now, okay? I can't deal with that and this at the same time."

She nods but doesn't look me in the eye, whispering "Okay" as she pulls away from the curb.

Once we pull into the mortuary parking lot, my legs feel like rubber. I close my eyes and take a few deep breaths. Jessica reaches for my hand and only let's go of it long enough to get out of the car. Thankfully, my parents have already pre-purchased their plots. It's just a matter of the casket, headstone, service details, and of course payment. Just a matter of... *Like this isn't the hardest thing I've ever had to do in my entire life.*

As we go through the motions, Jessica prompts me and helps answer most of the questions. It's decided it'll be a closed casket for obvious reasons. Bob, the funeral director, has a few more questions. I can't help but think how creepy his fucking job is. Walking around dead people all day, talking about dead people all day, planning goodbyes for dead people all day—it gives me the creeps. At the same time, I'm grateful that people like Bob are around because you really have to want to help people to do his job. I feel like maybe I should give him a big tip for doing it all. Do you tip funeral directors? I have no fucking clue but it seems like it should be a highly tippable industry.

"Mr. Matthews, will there be a photo montage for your father?"

Suddenly, it hits me. *I'm now Mr. Matthews.* The *only* Mr. Matthews. I blink back the tears. *I will not break here.*

"No."

"Okay, no problem. I understand. I think we've worked out all the details except the music. Your mother said on the phone she had some specific requests. Do you have them?"

Can't forget the fucking music, as if we'll even be paying attention to it. I know I plan on blocking the day permanently from my memories. "Yes, *Amazing Grace.* Any church version will do. *Bridge Over Troubled Water,* the Michael Smith version. Also, Eric Clapton's *Tears in Heaven* and *You Raise Me Up* by Josh Groban. I'm sorry to be abrupt but are we done here now? I really need to be getting back to my mother."

He stands apologetically, "Of course, Mr. Matthews. My assistant, Millie, will stop by this evening for the suit your father is to be buried in and then we'll be set for the services on Wednesday. I'm very sorry for your loss and if I can assist you with anything further please let me know."

I thank him and bolt outside for some air that doesn't smell like it's shrouded in death.

The car ride home is quiet, abnormally quiet. I don't think I've ever seen Jessica stay silent this long. When we pull into my driveway, she starts to get out of the car.

"Jessica, wait, don't bother getting out. I'm really not in the mood for company."

Biting down on her lip, she nods her head. "Okay, Michael, but wait please, for just a minute. The next few days are going to be hard for us all. I'm here for you, whatever you need. But when this is all over, if not before, you need to talk to Katie Grace. She didn't do what you accused her of, and I think you know that deep down. I know you don't want to talk about it, but she's not okay, Michael. If you thought she was bad when Lila died you should see her now. She was a fucking rainbow of sunshine back then compared to now."

My hands are balled into fists I can't listen to anymore. "ENOUGH, JESSICA! I said I didn't want to talk about it and I don't. I'm not thinking about her right now, I can't. I'll see you at the funeral if you choose to come, but tell Katherine I said to remember she isn't welcome."

I hear her crying as I slam the door, but I don't care; I'm too pissed off. It's hard to believe it was only two days ago I was going to ask Katherine to marry me. Storming through the front door, I go straight to my room and flop myself on my bed, reliving that day in my mind.

~~~***~~~

I was so close to asking her to marry me when the phone rang—just a few minutes more and it would have been a done deal. After I sent Katherine home from the hospital, she was all I could think of to keep my thoughts off the surgery. I really needed her there with me and was pissed to have to send her away. I passed the time praying and thinking of all the ways I could make that night up to her once my dad recovered. As hard as I tried, I couldn't figure out why my mom lost her shit on Katherine earlier. I knew how pissed and disappointed my dad would be when he found out my mom chased her off. A little while after I got to the hospital, Tom showed up. He was a friend and co-worker of my dad's. He and my mom had their heads together talking. All the while my anger was rapidly increasing as I dwelled on the fact that I was sitting there all alone but she was being nice and chummy with that asshole.

Finally, I just couldn't take it anymore. "Mom, what the hell? You need to talk to me."

Tom stood and tried to get in my face, "Son, you shouldn't ever speak to your mother like that."

Oh, the fuck he didn't. I got real close to him so he didn't mistake his place for a minute, "This is none of your god damned business. You should go, Tom, your presence isn't necessary or wanted here."

"Michael Matthews, mind your manners. I raised you better than this!"

"Are you fucking kidding me, Mom? This douchebag gets to be here, but you sent your daughter home? My almost wife can't be here, but he can? What in the fuck is going on around here?"

She broke down in tears and I felt like an ass. The love of her life was in critical condition; I knew I would be a mess if it was reversed. I knelt in front of her, shooting a warning glare to Tom to keep his motherfucking distance. "Mom, I'm sorry. I don't want you to cry. Please, just tell me what's going on."

As she wiped her tears with her tissue, she nodded her head in agreement. Before she had a chance to tell me anything, the doctor came in looking dejected and I knew in that instant he was gone. The words melted together, but I didn't need to hear them I knew what she was saying. My mom clutched on to me and unleashed every sadness and heartbreak contained within her.

It all happened so quickly but it seemed like hours. Tom took a seat on the other side of my mom and rested his head in his hands.

Suddenly, my need for Katherine overwhelmed me. I needed to feel her, to be with her. She was the only one that could fix me, the only one that would understand.

"Tom, can you please take my mom home?"

"Yes, of course, Michael."

My mom jumped up, trying to stop me from leaving. "No, Michael, wait, we have to talk first. Before you go back to Katherine you have to know everything. You can't be with that little bitch until you know the truth."

The venom in her words shot straight to my heart. "Mom! What the hell? Why are you on the 'I hate Katherine' train tonight?"

Her blue eyes blazed into mine with a determination I'd never seen before. "Because of this, Michael. Right here!"

She pulled a piece of paper out of her pocket that had my dad's handwriting on it. It was ripped in half and at the top it said 'suspects'. There were a few names I didn't recognize, but the bottom two names I did. Joseph and Katherine. I took a seat and tried to think calmly about it. It didn't mean anything. It was just a profile he was working off of. Since the bottom is missing there's no way to know what else was there.

"Mom, I get this looks bad but it doesn't mean anything. Katherine loved Dad. I wouldn't put any of this past Joseph but Katherine wouldn't have done it. Not in a million years."

She snickered at me, "Don't be so naïve. People have done much, much worse for money." She proceeded to tell me about the vote, the buyout, and his thoughts about the previous break in. But still, it wasn't enough to condemn her.

"I can see you're going to be just as hard to convince as I was. Listen to this voicemail Tom forwarded me earlier from Joseph, and then listen to the message he forwarded me from your dad."

I took my mom's phone with a bad feeling in the pit of my stomach. The first message was from Joseph to Tom. "It's done. Make sure the board is on top of this, I don't need any backlash coming my way. My daughter took care of the paperwork so there shouldn't be any loose ends."

Fuck. "When did you get this message, Tom?"

"Today, of course, when else?"

"Michael, listen to your father's message. It's important. It will... change everything."

I didn't want to hear his voice—it was going to break me—but I had to know. "Tom, it's Grant. I've been let go...Joseph must have done it...Katherine was there...at the house...I'm on my way to meet you...I can't believe she would do this...It's going to break him...I have to get to him...before it's too late."

Fuck me, it was true. Even though every third word cut in and out, I got the general message. Katherine took the contract from the house and gave it to Joseph. My dad was trying to find me and stop me from proposing. Well, he managed that alright, just not in the way he'd planned.

I had to get out of there. I couldn't breathe. "Tom, take her home. I've got to go."

"Michael, wait!"

I was so pissed at her; it wasn't her fault but I had to direct it somewhere. "No, Mom, I have to go. I'll see you back at the house tomorrow. I have to go deal with this. You got what you wanted—I waited, I listened, and you wrecked my entire god damn life with a piece of paper and two voicemails. Are you fucking happy? You could have let this go, you could have kept this from me, but instead you chose to wreck me! Just because your life was annihilated tonight doesn't mean you had to annihilate mine, too! This could all be circumstantial still—that last message was choppy and the first one could have been anything. I have to go, I have to think. Don't call me, don't reach out. I'm not interested."

I walked around for a little while but I had to see Katherine. That didn't really help because I cried myself to sleep in the warmth of her welcoming arms. By morning, I was filled with rage and I couldn't make it go away. All night, I dreamt of my dad and kept hearing those messages play over and over in my head, along with my mom and Tom's words, and I was finally convinced Katherine had done this to him, to us, and my heart couldn't take another loss. Instead of processing my hurt, I turned it into rage and it felt so good to lash out at her. It felt so good to see her crying and begging. Knowing how much pain I was inflicting and how deep those daggers were reaching inside of her continued to fuel my fire.

I left her there in tears and I walked for hours until I finally caught a cab home. I'd always gotten mad easily. Always been overprotective of those I loved, especially Katherine, but that rage was new and I didn't know what to do with it. I'd lost my dad, the love of my life, most likely Jessica and honestly, I really didn't feel the need to keep my mom close anymore, either. I couldn't even begin to process what I felt because I just needed to get away from it all. I'd give it until after the funeral, go home and take care of it all, but if nothing changed, if my feelings didn't change, I was leaving and cutting everyone off until I straightened my shit out. It was the only way.

I paused before walking into the house, knowing that he wouldn't be there. Every part of my being wanted to get back in that cab and flee. Instead of calling the cab back, I opened the door to face the showdown that I knew was coming.

I walked into the kitchen to get some water and found my mom at the table, presumably drunk. There was a nearly empty bottle of vodka next to her. She was buried knee deep in what was likely every picture of my dad ever taken. She was torturing herself.

"Well, look who decided to grace me with his presence. You finally managed to take a break from the tramp, did you?"

She was going to make me lose my shit, I knew it. Claire Matthews could be described as a lot of things, but a nice drunk wasn't one of them. "Stop it, Mom. You're not the only one hurting right now."

She snickered at me, "No, maybe not, but I'm not the one fucking the person who killed your father, either."

"God damn it, Claire, fucking drop it, will you?! We just lost Dad; I can't deal with this right now."

She flung herself out of the chair, stumbling to get closer to me "Since when do you call your mother by her first name? You will show me some respect in my home, damn it. I'm painfully aware that we just lost your father. The love of my life is gone forever because of that little bitch and her father. Michael, this isn't a choice you get to make. It's done. You have to break it off with her. You'll never be happy, not now. Even if your heart doesn't want to accept it, you can't deny the evidence. I thought she was Lila through and through but Katherine is the epitome of her father. God help us all."

Closing my eyes, I counted to ten because if I didn't, I might have killed her with my bare hands. "Mother, don't worry. It's over, done, never to be spoken of again. I'm not with her anymore and never will be. You can knock that smile off your face because I'm done with you, too. I'll make the funeral arrangements and get you through the services, but after that I'm leaving. I can't live here in your house, especially without Dad. I'm over it. I need a fresh start and that involves leaving everyone I know in the past. I've made it very clear to Katherine that neither she nor Joseph is welcome at the funeral."

I ducked as she threw her glass over my head and it shattered against the wall. She was ranting and raving and it's a mixture of pain, loss and fear. I never thought I would come to a point where I would cut her out of my life, but it was all too much. I watched her carefully as she went from her rage to hysterics. I tried to help her but she kicked and screamed at me so I called the doctor to come and sedate her. As I put her in bed, she reached out, clutching my wrist. She could barely form words between the alcohol and the shot. I was surprised she could say anything at all.

"Michael, I wish it wasn't this way. I loved her, too. This hurts me, too, but it's what your father believed, it's what he wanted for you. Please don't leave me. I can't be alone; it's too hard."

With the last word that fell from her lips, her hand released mine and she passed out. The finality of her statement hit me hard. It was what my father wanted. I could honor his wishes even if it killed me. If he believed it, it must be true.

Carefully closing the door, I exited the room,
praying she'd find some peace in her sleep.

~~~***~~~

The next few days passed in a blur—fielding phone calls, talking to lawyers, avoiding Jessica and Katherine—my life was a mess. I was finally beginning to understand why Katherine pulled inside of herself in order to not have to deal with people.

My mom and I rode in absolute silence to the funeral. There were many people there but I was thankful that Joseph and Katherine were nowhere in sight. Jessica was next to me the entire time, holding my hand, but we never spoke. She tried to corner me at the wake but she must have been able to tell from the look on my face it wasn't time to talk. As she left, she hugged me something fierce and told me she would be back in a few days to talk. I felt a flood of relief knowing that in a few days I would be gone and able to avoid that entire conversation.

My mom's sister, Dot, flew in for the funeral. She was recently divorced and doesn't look like she's coping well, either. I was able to convince her to come and stay with my mom for a while, figuring it would be good for both of them. They've always been close, but don't see each other as often as they'd like. I finally feel like I can leave and not be completely abandoning my mother. Claire Matthews is strong; she'll bounce back and start kicking some ass eventually. I have no doubt about that.

As for me, I just need to find myself and I'll never be able to do that here. College was never in the cards for me but I want to find out who I am. Unfortunately, it took a few weeks to tie up all the loose ends instead of the few days I originally anticipated and I didn't get to leave right after the funeral. Turns out, there was more money than I originally thought. Joseph wasn't such a heartless prick after all; he hadn't canceled the life insurance. Must have been his guilty conscious getting to him, whatever the reason it makes things much easier. I don't feel nearly as bad now for leaving my mom. I transferred all my assets back to my mom and only kept ten grand and my car. I figured that would be a good starting point, but the rest I want to figure out on my own.

I've successfully put Jessica off for a few weeks, but she is getting less and less patient with me. I still never let her talk about Katherine. I packed some essentials, photos, and Katherine's ring to take with me. Even though I was pissed as hell at her, I couldn't leave every trace of her in the past, not yet. My mom knows I'm leaving but not when. She's out with Dot, so I left her a note. It's easier this way. Unfortunately for me, as I put the last box in my car, Jessica pulls up and she's in a rage like I've never seen. She doesn't look like herself. She's got bags under her eyes, no makeup on, and looks as if she hasn't been eating much.

"What the hell is going on, Matthews? Damn it! I've given you space, but enough is enough. You don't return calls or texts? For the love of God, I *need* to talk to you!"

I lean against my car and meet her glare with one of my own. I know I have to tell her I'm leaving and it's not going to go over well.

"Maybe you should take that as a hint then, Jessica. I don't want to talk to anyone. I don't want to be around anyone. I don't want a fucking guilt trip from you and I sure as fuck don't want to talk about Katherine. Look, I'm leaving anyway. I have to get away from here and figure out my life."

She's stunned into silence. *That's a first.* Finally, she speaks so softly I have to get right next to her to even hear her words.

"You have no idea what this is like. *None.* You two are my best friends and I'm losing you both in different ways. She told me what you *think* happened and I don't know why you would think that about her. I can only imagine you have your reasons but I can tell you it's not true. I've never seen someone fall apart in front of my eyes but I'm scared, Michael. I think I'm going to have to have her committed. Now you're telling me you're leaving us? Leaving her for good? Leaving *me*? The Three Musketeers, remember? No matter what. I *know* we can fix this. You just have to talk to me, Michael… *please* talk to me. I'm all alone here. I need you. I need my best friend to help me through this. If it's really something you guys can't work through, we'll figure it out, but don't abandon me, Michael. Please. I don't have anyone else, just you."

"Wait here a minute. I need to grab something, I'll be right back."

I run inside and grab Wally. Jessica can take him home and maybe in some small way he can help Katherine since I can't.

"Here, make sure Katherine gets Wally." I push him into her arms but she just stares at me in disbelief.

"That's all you have to say? That's all you have to offer? I know you're grieving, and I'm trying to give you space, I really am, but I'm desperate and Wally is *not* going to help this time."

The tears are streaming down her face and I feel like the world's biggest asshole. I know we can't all be friends anymore and I could never put Jessica in the middle of us. This is my final gift to Katherine. She needs Jessica more than I do, and from the sounds of it, more than ever. The tiny piece of me that wants to believe what she's saying is dying inside as I listen to her describe Katherine's condition. But the rest of me, the angry part of me, couldn't give a flying fuck. I know if I'm going to shake Jessica, this has to be permanent. I have to be the asshole in this situation.

"Look, Jessica, I wish things could have been different but they're not. I wish I didn't know the things about her that I do, but I'm not going to taint you with them. You guys were friends first, and you'll be friends always, but you and I are done. I'm done with both of you. Both of us can't have you, so I'm giving you to her."

"That's not your fucking decision to make, you asshole!"

Oh, she's pissed now. Good. That should make this easier. "Yes, Jessica, actually it is. I'm removing myself from the equation so there is no alternative. Don't feel bad, I'm cutting off everyone, not just you two. Maybe someday I'll be ready to come back and deal with it when I get my head on straight, but today's not that day. When I get to where I'm going, I'm changing my number, so don't bother trying to get ahold of me."

"You can't do that."

"I can and I will. It's easier this way, trust me. I'm doing you a favor. You don't want to be around the person I am right now. This is best for all of us."

She snickers at me, "You've always been a domineering prick, haven't you? I used to think you were protecting Katie Grace, helping her cope and deal. You unilaterally brought her back from Lila's death and she's been under your thumb ever since. She's right where you wanted her, right where you like her, enraptured by you *and* your love. But now that the tables are turned, she's not allowed to fix *you*, to help *you* heal. Maybe you're right, Michael, maybe we'll both be better off without you. Just mark my words, I'm going to make it my mission to find her a man that will treat her as an equal and not make decisions for her. Who knows? Maybe it just might even be Marc."

She looks at me smugly, knowing that he's my weakness, but I won't let her know she got to me. She has to believe this is the end. If she believes it, she can convince Katherine of it, too.

I nod my head at her, getting ready to lie to her for the very first time in my life. "You're right, Jessica, I'm a domineering prick. Just ask Riley, she's all too used to my domineering ways. I had to have someone to fuck on the side who could take it rough. Katie Grace needed to be made love to gently, slowly, and passionately, but Riley let me fuck her like a real man. Now I don't have to juggle them and the relief from that is liberating. If Marc wants her, he can have her, but from what I've heard about him, she's a little too timid for his tastes. You never know, though, maybe he'll change for her or figure out how to bring out her inner freak, God knows I never coul…"

Before I finish my sentence, she slaps me across the face. I absolutely deserve it, but the look on her face says it all—I have effectively closed the door with her.

"You bastard!"

"Goodbye, Jessica. Have a nice life."

As I pull out of the driveway, I see her hunched over her steering wheel, chest heaving up and down as she sobs so loudly I still hear her four houses away. I wish she wasn't in the middle and that I didn't have to hurt her, too. *It's for the best, I know it is.*

Part Two

What Comes After

I haven't thought about my past like this in years. It hurts a lot, especially when I think about how stupid I was throwing away the best part of my life. Remembering when I asked her to be my girlfriend and how easy it was to tell her I loved her that night really hits home. I've never told anyone but her that I love them. Most couples have to wait at least a few months to say those words, but not us. We had love for each other before we ever considered a relationship. I think that's what made our relationship so special…it thrived off of that love.

That's why I know she can't love Daniel, even if she thinks she does. Kate isn't built that way—she doesn't love that fast. She takes her time so that she can get to know people and learn about them. This is a case of lust, plain and simple. Daniel, on the other hand, he falls hard and fast, but after Vanessa I didn't think he would let that happen again. He was so jaded after that and yet Kate pulled him out of his funk and brought him back to life.

This is a good start; I can use all of this when I explain our relationship to Daniel. I have to make him understand that Kate and I are meant to be.

Chapter 8 ~ New Beginnings

It's been a week since I left Jessica crying in my driveway. Every day that passes is another one further away from the biggest mistake of my life. Finally, I know what it means when people say 'If you haven't walked in my shoes, you'll never understand my journey' because it's true. Ever since the night of the accident I've been constantly at war with my emotions. I can't stop thinking about what Jessica said. *Especially* the parts about me being domineering and keeping Katherine under my thumb all these years. I've tried to reconcile my actions in my head, tried to justify my anger with Marc and my need to keep Katherine safe from pain. Ultimately, I'm the one that caused her the most pain. I was the one that shattered her beyond fixing. I've spent nine years keeping her safe from pain only to be the one to hurt her most. It's unforgivable.

All I needed was some time away to clear my head. I quickly came to the realization that Katherine couldn't have done what my dad thought she did. There are just too many inconsistencies—the messages sounded forced, the paper was ripped right at her name, and *all* of the information came from Tom. I've never liked Tom, and wouldn't trust him to feed my fish let alone with important messages. Even so, I can't bring myself to go back and clear up the misunderstanding, either. I believe things will be better this way. She deserves more than I can give her. Seeing the pain in her eyes that I put there would break me, and there's still the Joseph factor. I wouldn't put any of it past *him*. So, I've been driving up the coast, taking in the sights, trying to clear my head for days. Thanks to my flawless fake ID, I've been able to be drunk at night and pass out without having to think. I know drinking isn't the answer, and I'll eventually have to get my shit together, but for the time being… it numbs everything.

For nineteen years, I've lived the life my parents wanted me to. I've loved the same girl for twelve of them. It's very possible I never developed my own sense of self. Essentially, Katherine and I were one from a very young age. I've thought a lot about the random talks I had with my dad about playing the field. He never actually *told* me to do it, but looking back, I wonder if he wasn't hinting that I should. I know he loved Katherine and wanted us together, but maybe he wanted *me* to be sure that Katherine was really the one. I would have never considered it before, but… maybe I should have. At this point, I've got nothing to lose.

~~~***~~~

Another week passes by as I roam around aimlessly and spend money I don't have to spend. I'm hungry and tired so I pull up to a coffee house in Brentwood. While approaching the counter, the two girls working are full of giggles as they not so subtly sneak looks at me. It isn't unusual for girls to pay attention to me. What is unusual is that I've never been in a position where I would consider giving them the time of day before. I decide to let this ride out and see where it goes. *A little harmless flirting can't hurt. It might even help me decide if I'm being stubborn by not trying to fix things with Katherine.*

"Hi! I'm Aimee and this is Julie. What can we get for you?" Aimee is blushing but Julie's looking at me like I'm her favorite candy.

"Hello, ladies, I'm Mike."

"Hi, Mike," they reply in unison.

"I'd like a café latte with four raw sugars and a bacon breakfast sandwich. Can I also get a bottle of water, please?"

I give Julie my credit card, and when she passes it back to me, she deliberately slides her fingers across mine. It's been a long time since I've been touched by another woman who wants my attention. It doesn't feel bad but it doesn't feel right, either. It's not that she's not attractive—she definitely is—she just isn't my typical type of girl. Julie has short, black hair with bright blue tips, at least six piercings in her ear and one in her nose. She's tall and thin. Everything about her is the exact opposite of Katherine. *Maybe opposite can be a good thing.*

"Go have a seat, Mike. One of us will bring you your order when it's up." She hasn't stopped smiling since she introduced herself. I smile back and head over to a table in the back corner. Aimee is the one to deliver my order along with a handwritten note.

"Here's your order, Mike. I'm having a huge party tonight for my birthday. We were hoping you might be able to come by. No presents or anything, just a reason for a bunch of college kids to have a party. I wrote down my address and my cell for you if you want to come."

Aimee seems like a sweet girl, a little more reserved than Julie for sure. She's pretty in a conservative way—simple makeup, brown hair and eyes, and adorable dimples. "Thanks for the invitation, Aimee, and Happy Birthday. I'm just passing through town but I'll think about it, okay? If I'm still here, I'll try and stop by."

"That would be great, Mike! I've got to get back to work but hopefully we'll be seeing you tonight. If not, whenever you come back into town don't hesitate to give me a call." She flashes me a sweet smile and waves as she heads back to work.

After leaving the coffee shop, I spend most of the day driving around, getting a feel for the city. Eventually, I'll have to settle down somewhere. I try and tell myself it has nothing to do with that fact that Katherine's condo isn't too far from where I am. After picking up some food from a deli, I drive to a nearby secluded park I found. While growing up, Katherine and I would sit at the table under the big oak tree at the park by our houses and talk for hours. I would sit on top of the table and she would sit between my legs, leaning against me. Looking back, I realize how mature we were for our age, we always were. Maybe we're old souls, or maybe we just grew up too fast when Lila died. Whatever the reason, Katherine and I always seemed to have deep, meaningful conversations. It was during one of these moments that I knew without a doubt that I wanted to spend the rest of my life with her. It was shortly after I started looking for her ring.

"Michael, do you think that our souls are attached to another soul when we're born? Not even just then, but if you believe that we're reborn

over and over do you think you're always attached to another soul?"

That was an interesting idea for sure. "I don't know, Katherine, maybe? But if so, I wonder if sometimes when people come back things get mixed up or lost in translation somehow. You see, people go their entire lives never finding the one."

She took my hand and placed it over her heart. "Then you need to memorize the way my heart beats because I don't want anything to get lost in translation. You never know what can happen. I don't know if I believe in soul mates for life as far as true love goes, but I do believe we have them for friendship. I know without a doubt you found me just when I needed you to."

I felt her heart pounding under my hand, the warmth seeping into my palm and I knew unequivocally that I would marry her one day. I pulled her into my lap and placed her hand over my heart.

"Do you feel that? The way my heart is racing? That's what you do to me, it's all you. I will love you until the day I die, Katie Grace, and then I'll come back and find you all over again, I promise." I watched as her eyes filled with amazement and tears, but before she had a chance to speak I pulled her in for a kiss that put all of our other kisses to shame.

Never would I have guessed we would end up where we are at this moment. Remembering that conversation is painful and eye opening. Regardless of what has happened in the past few weeks, we both need time to grow. We were wrapped in a bubble for years and now we've finally emerged. We need to grow up apart before we can come back together. If we are truly soul mates, we'll still find our way back to each other. I want to be a better man for her but I need to get past the hurt and anger of everything that has come between us. I know it's irrational but a big part of me still blames her for this mess I'm in. I need to live for *me* for a change. More importantly, she needs to figure out who she is without me. Even though I know this is the right path for both of us, it pisses me off. It isn't what I wanted, and I don't want to feel the kind of pain I'm feeling now ever again.

When I leave the park, I pass some time watching a movie. I'm trying to avoid renting another hotel room because I'm running out of money, but it's not exactly comfortable trying to sleep in a Porsche. Selling my car and buying something cheaper that would give me some money to live off of for a while has crossed my mind several times. I never realized how hard it is to fill your time when you don't have a home to go to. At only 10 pm, I'm bored and tired of being alone. I decide to go check out Aimee's party. First stop, the liquor store for two large bottles of Patron. At the very least, I'll be able to get drunk and pass out on her floor. I text her and let her know I'm coming to the party after all.

Their neighborhood is nice, with large houses. They're not as big as ours were growing up, but they look close. Finally, I find a place to park down the street and walk up to the house. Julie and Aimee are waiting for me out front and are most definitely drunk already.

"Mike! You came to my party *and* you brought tequila. You are the man of our dreams!"

I laugh at her; she's a cute drunk. "You mean the man of *your* dreams, don't you?"

"No, she definitely means *our* dreams, don't you, baby?" Julie leans in and pulls Aimee into a kiss that would rival any porn I've seen. It's hot.

"So, you two are…"

Julie cuts me off by pulling me in for a kiss which is incredibly hot and makes me feel like an ass all at the same time. "We don't put labels on our relationship. We're open to lots of things, but tonight we're looking for a third. You game?"

I'm floored. I was totally not expecting my night to end up like this. No guy in his right mind would turn them down. But I'm not exactly in my right mind. "Look, I'm just getting out of a really long-term relationship. I don't know if this is the best idea right now."

Aimee pulls me in for a kiss. Running her hands under my shirt, she wraps her arms around me and pulls me in deeper. Her chest is pushed up against mine and the feeling of her hard nipples has my dick standing at attention. When she breaks away, she looks up at me with longing in her eyes. "Mike, we don't want a commitment, we just want to have fun. Let us help you forget, even if it's just for tonight."

Ah hell, there's no way I can turn that down.

We break open the Patron and take more shots than I can count before taking the party to a bedroom.

A few hours later, both girls are passed out and wrapped around each other, naked. I stumble out of the room and into the backyard. My thoughts are reeling as I collapse in a chair under a tree. That was the hottest, most erotic thing I have ever seen, let alone *done*. As amazing as it was, I feel sick inside. I can *never* go back to Katherine's bed after doing that. There's still people partying, looks like this one will go all night. I really want to leave, but I'm too drunk to drive. I feel so lost. Dropping my head into my hands, I sit there for I don't even know how long.

"Hey, are you doing okay over here? You've been out here for a while. Can I get you a drink or something?"

Great. I must look like a total loser sitting here with my head in my hands. Two guys take a seat in the chairs across from me. "Yeah, I'm okay, just out here thinking."

They exchange a look that I wouldn't call pity, but I can tell they're curious about the drunk guy outside all alone.

"I'm Daniel, and this is my friend, Connor. We live next door and go to school with Aimee. Do you go to UCLA, too?"

Fuck this is a UCLA party? The last thing I need is to bump into Jessica or Katherine here. It really isn't Katherine's scene, but I could see Jessica dragging her along, trying to get her to meet new people. "No, I'm just passing through town. I met Aimee at the coffee shop today and she invited me. I'm Mike."

Connor laughs, "So *you* were their third tonight. They were wondering if you were going to come. Or should I say show? If you're here, you *definitely* came. No wonder you're out here alone, you're recovering. They can be a bit overwhelming, in a sinfully delicious way."

Daniel raises his hands up and laughs. "Don't look at me, I wouldn't know. They haven't been able to talk me into that yet. Maybe someday, but then again…maybe not. You look like they've put you through the ringer tonight and not in a good way."

"Oh no, they were fine, shit, *more* than fine. That was the hottest thing ever. I've just got some stuff going on and I'm trying to figure out when life is going to stop shitting on me. Hell, maybe it's perspective. Maybe I just keep jumping into a shithole head first with no way out." Why I'm sitting here, talking to these guys about my life I have no idea. It's probably because I'm drunk and lonely enough to talk to strangers. It's not like I have any friends anymore. Even if I make a fool out of myself, I'll never have to see these guys again.

"You said you were passing through town. Maybe when you get home you'll have a different perspective on things. Shit storms have to end sometime. Just ask Connor, he starts a hell of a lot of them."

"Fuck you, dude. Girls jump in headfirst and don't know how to dig their way out. I've never said anything to lead a girl on. They just read between nonexistent lines. If that's what's going on with you, Mike, I got your back."

"No, not exactly. The bottom line is that some serious shit went down at home and I lost someone very close to me. My long-term girlfriend and I broke up because she did some pretty unforgivable things...or so I thought. I'm not even sure anymore. I wasn't exactly nice to her, either. It's not something we can come back from, *especially* after tonight. We lived in the same town, had the same friends, and practically shared families, so I left. I've been living out of hotels and my car for the past few weeks, trying to figure out what's next. I was supposed to go to UCLA, but that wasn't my dream. Tonight was just an escape, but now it's over, and once I sober up I need to figure out what's next."

"That's messed up. It definitely sounds like a shit storm, not a head first jump into shit."

I laugh. At least *someone* seems to be on my side.

"Well, why don't you come over and crash at our house until you sober up? Connor's brother, Jake, is away for the weekend with his fiancée. You can crash in his room. From the look on your face, I think it's a better alternative than going back in and curling up with Julie and Aimee. Not that they'd get attached, I've never seen them with a repeat yet."

That makes me chuckle, "Yeah, I can't see them as the kind of girls looking to be attached. If you guys really don't mind, it would be nice to crash somewhere other than my car for the night."

"Cool, let's go before they come out here and try to talk Daniel into staying. Seriously, dude, I don't know how you keep turning them down."

Daniel just shakes his head, "Not my thing I guess, at least not now."

You gotta respect a guy who can say no. I probably should've said no, too. There's no going back now, but it *was* a pretty incredible night. Maybe it's time to play the field. It was nice to have my thoughts occupied by something other than Katherine for a change.

I take a look around as we walk into their house. It's definitely a bachelor pad. Where there should've been a dining table there's a pool table instead. Black leather couches, two recliners, and a coffee table are basically it for furniture. It's a pretty open floor plan. There's a table in the kitchen which is covered in beer cans, cards, and what looks to be two bikini tops.

"Looks like you guys had some fun earlier yourselves," I say, nodding my head toward the kitchen.

"Yeah, well Aimee and Julie's parties are known for attracting women who want to have a good time. They don't have them often, but when they do we usually benefit some."

"Connor benefits the most. This is the first time I haven't been in a relationship for a while. Jake never benefits but he doesn't want to. His fiancée, April, is the kind of woman you would be a fool to turn away. They've been together since high school. He's a lucky bastard. So, you want to play a game or do you want to call it a night?"

"Sure, I'm up for a game."

Connor yawns, "Sorry, guys, count me out. I'm exhausted and I have to meet my parents for breakfast in the morning. Stick around if you want to, Mike, Jake won't be back until Sunday. We can barbecue and kick it by the pool."

"Sounds good, I'll think about it. Thanks."

Daniel and I stayed up playing for a few hours and shot the shit. He's a pretty cool guy. He mentioned that his family owns a construction company and that they're hiring. He told me to think about if I was interested and we could talk more about it later. It's an interesting idea. I've always been intrigued by building things and by architecture and I *need* a job. The more I think about it, I know I want to do it. He said the position would be back out toward Santa Barbara which is good. Anything to help keep me away from L.A. is exactly what I'm looking for.

Chapter 9 ~ Getting to Know You

A month has passed since I met Daniel and Connor and things are good. I stayed the weekend with them after the party and Daniel brought me out to meet his parents. Rick is tough but he's fair. Bev is so warm and loving; they remind me of my parents. Rick offered me a job but let me know that in no uncertain terms would he tolerate anyone who wasn't serious about learning the business. It's ball busting work but I love it. It doesn't leave me much time to think, either. At work I'm focused, and when I get home, I'm so exhausted that the only place I think of Katherine is in my dreams. I traded my Porsche in for a truck and moved in with Bev and Rick. I love it here. Bev tells me stories of all the kids growing up and how it was for her and Rick when they were young.

Bev's the kind of person who can draw out your all your inner secrets. She doesn't judge, she just listens. I told her about Katherine and my dad. I explained to her why it's so important to me to figure out who I am without her before I can talk to her again. She seemed to understand all too well the pain that comes with heartache. It was nice to vent my anger and frustrations to someone and she promised she wouldn't tell anyone what I've been dealing with.

Daniel's been coming up each weekend to visit his parents but I have a feeling he's also making sure things are working out with me here. After all, he *did* essentially drop a stranger into his parents' lap. When he comes up we go to the site and he gives me some additional training. It's been really helpful and they already trust me with more work than the guys that started the same time I did. Daniel's a talker. I haven't been around a lot of guys that talk as much as he does. He's the type of guy that really wants to get to know people. Katherine would have really liked him; he has a lot of her characteristics. They both really have a way connecting with the people around them, but never in a pushy way. He obviously cares about people since he basically just saved a virtual stranger from self-destruction.

Tonight they're having a party at the house and invited me to come down. I'm still a little hesitant to be there since they go to UCLA. But I can't let my life revolve around my proximity to Katherine and Jessica. I'm living my life for me now.

My job is to pick up the kegs on the way, which is much easier to do with my new truck. I also grabbed a couple of bottles of Absolute. I figure maybe I should stay away from the tequila tonight. I make sure to arrive early since I have the beer. I carry the vodka in the house first and am literally attacked by a gorgeous girl. She's not my typical type, but hot damn, she's got curves in all the right places. I *definitely* wouldn't kick her out of *my* bed.

She puts her arm through mine, leading me into the kitchen. "I don't know who you are, but you, my friend, are my new favorite person. Finally, a man that understands not all girls like tequila!"

It's hard not to notice that I'm being glared at hard, presumably by Jake. He looks like a larger version of Connor. I then make the connection that the beautiful vixen draped across my arm must be April. Placing the bottles on the table, I extricate myself from her grasp.

Reaching out my hand to introduce myself, I can tell he doesn't give a fuck who I am. "Hi, I'm Mike, you must be Jake and April." Jake crosses his arms over his chest and looks me up and down from head to toe. I'm not one to be intimated by anyone, but this guy is built. I have no doubt he could and would squash me like a piss ant. He's obviously very possessive of his fiancée. He finally nods his head but doesn't say a single word. *Great.*

"Oh stop it, Jake! I'm friendly, get over it. He's a friend, you big oaf. I'm so tired of you being so territorial." She points to the ring on her finger, "Remember this? This means I'm yours now and always. Even without this ring I never stood a chance and neither did you. Promise ring or not, you're all I need. Now stop being an ass and say hi to Mike."

Jake pulls April in close, her back against his chest, and wraps his arms around her as he kisses the top of her head. He finally cracks a smile, even if she can't see it. I get the impression he likes it when she gets a little bossy. "Hey."

"Pffft. That's better I guess. Mike, it's nice to finally meet you, Daniel's told us a lot about you. You're right, I'm April, and this territorial ass, is my fiancé, Jake. You can just call him my personal security detail because once I start drinking he'll be following me around all night."

I crack a smile at her, I like them. Actually, she kind of reminds me of Jessica.

"Damn straight I will be. Did you see the way he eye fucked you when he came in? And he's a 'friend', so all the guys that come here tonight that aren't 'friend' status won't stop with just the eye fucking they'll be persistent. That means I'll have to kick some asses. I trust you, babe, but when you drink you're *extra* friendly. Even if your intentions are pure, theirs may not be. Besides, you get horny when you're drunk and I want to be right next to you to soak up all that sexual fun. Come on, Mike, let me help you get the kegs out of the car."

April stretches on her tiptoes and gives him a kiss as he walks away.

"One and only warning, *friend*. We'll be cool as long as I never see you eye fuck my girl again. Got it?"

Yeah, loud and clear. "Sure, that's not my thing, man. I wouldn't ever try to mess with someone else's girl, that's not cool. You've got nothing to worry about."

"Alright then, we're cool."

It didn't take long for the party to get in full swing after we unloaded the kegs. I guess Jake decided he trusted me enough to leave April with me while he grilled some food. Daniel and Connor are inside playing a raging game of beer pong. April wasn't kidding about her love for vodka.

She's slurring her words after a bit. Jake notices, too, so he brings her a plate of food.

"Hi, baby!" April jumps up and throws her legs around his waist. Thankfully, he passed the plate to me right before she did. She obviously has no issues dry humping him in front of everyone but Jake has other plans. He gently pulls away and sets her back in her chair, kneeling in front of her.

"April, will you do something for me, please?"

The look she gives him is pure adoration; I've seen that look before in a different set of eyes. I need another shot; I'm not going there tonight.

"Of course, Jake, what do you need?"

"I need you to eat, baby. I don't want you passing out on me before I even finish the food. Then later, I'm going to take you upstairs and lock us in my room."

"Jake, I'm not hungry and I can't go to bed until Lexi gets here. I want to introduce her to Mike!"

Jake shakes his head at me, "Mike, you *do not* want to go there. Trust me, dude, Lexi is extra friendly to everyone she meets and if you give her an inch she's a stage five clinger."

"That's Jake's nice way of saying that she's a tramp. But, Mikey, you *need* a rebound and Lexi can be a good one. If you don't want her to cling, don't act like you like her. Make sure she knows it's just fun. She's cool if she knows, it's when guys act like they like her and use her that she clings."

I laugh and so does Jake, "Oh baby, now I know how drunk you *really* are. You just told a guy how to avoid a crazy Lexi when usually you say they deserve what they get. This is priceless. No more shots for you. I want to enjoy you. Give me twenty minutes and then I'm taking you to bed."

"I'm not, not *that* much anyway, intoxicated I mean. I mean I'm not a drunk, not drunk. Whatever, you know what I mean. Hurry up and take me to bed, Jake. I need you right now." Damn, the look she gives him almost makes *me* hard.

Jake groans, "Mike, watch her like a hawk. I'll be back in five minutes. I'm going to have Daniel take over the grill." I nod as he walks away.

"Take a shot with me, Mike. Oh look, there's Lexi! Whoo hooo, Lexi, over here, girl!" *Oh man, she's so drunk.* Lexi waves at her and heads our way. She's cute, but even I have to admit that she's got a 'fuck me' vibe to her. April jumps up and tackles her in a big hug.

"Lexi, this is my new friend, Mike. Mike this is Lexi. Can I have a shot now, please?" I laugh at her; I think I love drunk April.

"How about I make you a deal? You eat the food Jake brought you, and I'll give you a shot afterward." Her bottom lip pokes out in a pout and she pokes her index finger into my chest.

"Fine, Mr. Mike, but you and Lexi have to drink while I eat. She's got some catching up to do." Lexi shrugs as if she doesn't care one way or the other. I'm just glad April is going to eat and I'm sure Jake will be, too.

"Okay, April, whatever you want. Lexi, is vodka okay with you?"

"Sure, I'm fine with whatever. I haven't seen you around before, are you a new student, Mike?" After taking her shot, she slowly licks her bottom lip then bites on it. It's hot and my dick hardens when I picture her lips wrapped around it.

"No, he's not a student. He works with Daniel, with the dad, with Mr. Daniel. Fuck it, you know what I mean." *Oh god, she's so funny drunk.* I just want to hug her but I wouldn't want Jake to think I'm making a move on her again. Connor's staggering toward us and it's obvious that he's pretty drunk, too. *Guess I know who lost beer pong.* April puts her plate down and hugs him hard.

"Connor! I love you so much, you're the best brother ever, my brother." He's laughing so freaking hard at her.

"April, you're drunk! I love drunk April. I love sober April, too, but I *really* love drunk April. Wanna play a game?"

"Yes! What kind of game?" Jake approaches and a stormy look crosses his face "No way, Connor, she's not playing games with you." He throws his arm over Jake's shoulder and knuckles his head. Jake does *not* look happy.

"Stop, Jake, I *want* to play with Connor. What are we playing?" We all take a round of shots, even Jake who's only had beer all night.

"Oh great, here we go. April, are you sure, baby? You know Connor's games are usually only fun for him."

"Yup, I'm sure" Jake shakes his head, kisses her on the cheek, and sits down. "Watch and learn, Mike. This will be over quickly."

I'm intrigued and so is Lexi who's now sitting next to me pouring us all more shots. Connor takes April's hand and talks to her very seriously.

"Okay, sister in law, I need your help finding Bugs Bunny. He got loose in the yard and I don't want him to get hurt. We have to be quiet so we don't scare him, though." April's eyes enlarge and she nods in agreement. Jake groans and takes a shot; he obviously knows what's coming. Daniel joins us and follows our gazes as they search the yard.

"Are they looking for Bugs?"

"Yup," Jake answers, taking another shot. Daniel reaches for one, too, and takes a seat to get a view of the show. After about ten minutes they come back and down shots. Suddenly, Connor jumps up, "I see him!"

"Where? Where do you see him, Connor?" While she's distracted and turning in circles, Connor drops his pants and points to his ass. "Here he's right here, don't you see him?" April is so drunk she actually looks at his ass really closely.

"I don't see anything!"

"Damn woman, you must have scared him into the hole." Everyone laughs as Connor pulls up his pants, barely able to button them he's laughing so hard. At first April doesn't get it, but you can see the light bulb go off in her head as his trick finally dawns on her.

"You're such a jerk! I can't believe I just got all up close and personal with your ass, Connor, gross! When was the last time you washed that thing? Jake, why did you let me play with him? He's not nice to me. You're not a brother, Connor. I mean you're not *my* brother anymore. Well, you can be my brother but I don't love you anymore."

He just smiles at her, "You do *too* love me and I'm always your brother, but you're fun when you're drunk and when I'm drunk you're even funner." She drops into Jake's lap, wrapping her arms around his neck. They start kissing passionately and we all avert our eyes, trying not to pay attention. They have what Katherine and I had but it seems a little more effortless for them somehow.

"Come on, April, get your lips off my brother and tell me how much you love me so he can take you to bed. If you don't, I'm going to follow you and knock on the door all night until you do."

Jake breaks away from her and helps her stand up. "Tell him you love him so I can have my way with you and not have to kick his ass."

"Fine, I love you, Connor, but no more hunting for rabbits in your ass anymore. That's not cool." Jake leads her away, choking on his laughter, and leaves us all cracking up.

Lexi scoots closer to me and places her hand on my thigh. "Do you want to go somewhere and talk, Mike? Get to know each other better?" Lexi's a pretty girl, her long black curly hair and green eyes accentuate her pale skin. *I wonder if she likes it rough?* Jake said she was a stage five clinger but I bet that means she's willing to do a lot of things other girls aren't. *Shit, I'm drunk and I should just let this go, but the way she's looking at me screams 'fuck me'...*

I place my arm across her shoulders, pulling her in close. "Lexi, I'm drunk and horny. I don't want to go anywhere to talk. I want to take you in the house and fuck you senseless." She's biting that damn lip of hers again and her breathing is rapid. I've got her, I know it, and I use the knowledge to my advantage. Leaning in, I pull her lip out of her mouth with my teeth and bite down before releasing it. "Stop biting your lip, Lexi. That's my job tonight and it's not the only part of you I want to bite. Do you like it rough? I won't be gentle and I won't call you. I'm not looking for a relationship, Lexi. I'm looking for fun. Are you fun, baby?" I love watching her squirm. She's turned on; I can tell by the way she's squeezing her thighs together. I draw my gaze slowly from her thighs back up to her face. Her chest is heaving rapidly and her eyes are glazed over in lust. I own her right now and I'm ready to have some fun.

Daniel hands us both shots but he doesn't say anything, just smirks at me. After taking my shot, I stand up and hold my hand out to Lexi. "Are you coming?"

She pounds her shot, eyes glazed over with desire, and takes my hand. "I sure the fuck hope so… multiple times."

Thank god I wake up in an empty bed this morning. I thought I heard Lexi do the walk of shame out of here a few hours ago. Even though she had *nothing* to be ashamed of. That night with Julie and Aimee opened my eyes to a different aspect of sex. Since then I've probably watched too much porn, but then again, there really isn't such a thing as too much porn. I'm done with nice and gentle sex; it's far more fun this way. If I'm being honest with myself, I don't want to make love to anyone again. The only person I can ever picture myself making love to is Katherine.

The way Lexi's pussy clenched around my dick when she came was incredible. Her clit was pierced and she came over and over again. She wasn't joking when she said she wanted multiple orgasms. Now that I've seen girls have them, I don't know why I never tried sooner. If I could have given Katherine multiples, I probably would have never given her up. Nothing in the world felt better than Katherine coming around me.

Then suddenly, a memory from last night slams into me like a freight train. *Fuck no, god please tell me I didn't*. I scramble around, looking for my phone which has fallen to the floor and grab it pulling up my call log. FUCK. My last call was to Katherine at a little before two am. I wrack my brain, pacing and running my hands through my hair. *Damn it!* There are only three people that

I know numbers for by heart. My mom, Jessica, and Katherine. I need to calm down and think. Deep breath in and out. After about ten minutes I remember, and it isn't good.

Lexi and I had just finished. Holy hell, she was a screamer and it was hot. She rolled over and put her hand over my heart. It reminded me of Katherine at the park that day and I pushed her away. "What's wrong, baby?"

"I'm not your baby, Lexi. Remember I said this was a one-time thing. You should go. I can't be what you want."

I had no idea what time it was but someone was playing Gone by NSYNC and it sounded like it was coming from Connor's room. That was the last song Katherine and I danced to. It was putting me on edge. I just wanted to be alone.

"I can make you forget her, Mike, you just need to give me a chance."

I laughed at her. "That's impossible, Lexi, you can't forget about the person who owns your soul." She nodded and actually looked at me with more understanding than I deserved.

"Then do yourself a favor, Mike, and fix it. Trust me, the self-destruction and random hookups won't change anything. You'll hate yourself in the long run and you'll lose her forever. If you still have a chance, fix it while you still can." With a quick peck on my cheek, she rolled over and soon I heard her steady breathing... she'd fallen asleep. Was she right? I reached for my phone and dialed the number, but I didn't press the talk button. Glancing at the clock, I realized it was almost 2

am. She most likely would've been asleep and the call would go to voicemail. Then I figured I could just let her know I was okay and I missed her. It couldn't hurt. If she answered the phone, I was prepared to hang up. She wouldn't know it was me since I'd changed my number.

I hit talk and almost hung up but something stopped me—probably the liquid courage—but it felt wrong. I knew I shouldn't be calling the woman I loved while in bed with another. When her voicemail picked up, the sound of her voice wrapped me in warmth. My heart sped up and broke at the same time. I missed her so much. I knew I'd never stop missing her, I needed her. She brought my soul to life. Without her there to set my soul on fire, I was just a shell of who I used to be. It's what I deserved, though. I didn't deserve happiness but she did. She deserved every happiness life had to offer. When the tone beeped, I started talking.

"Katherine, it's Michael. I'm calling because I need to say a few things to you. I might be drunk, too. I'm sorry I left you like that. I'm sorry I couldn't control my temper and I treated you bad. I'm no good for you. Baby, I've done things these past few weeks I'm not proud of. Did you know I never wanted to go to school? That I was only going for you? No, you didn't because I never told you. I'm sure Jessica told you about Riley but I swear that wasn't true. I needed you both to let go. Don't wait around for me being miserable. I want you to be happy. Someday I'll come back because I need you, I'll always need you. I won't let things get lost in translation next time, I promise. I'll come back and find you when it's time. I need to truly forgive Joseph, my mom,

maybe you, and definitely myself. I need to get my head in a different space. I want to be someone better than I am now, for you, for us. When the time comes I'll have to tell you the things I've done and hope you'll find it in your heart to forgive me. I can imagine by then I'll have a lot to be forgiven for and I apologize in advance for that. Just know I love you. I've loved you since we were seven and I'll love you until I die. Then when I come back I'll find you all over again. I miss you, Katherine. The ache that your presence has been replaced with is a pain that should be reserved for someone deep in the depths of hell. Being without you is my own personal hell. Please don't call this number; I'll change it if you do. It's better this way. I don't have the right to ask, but please trust me when I say I need to become me before we can become an us again. Most importantly, I think you need to find you, too, Katherine Grace Moore. You're going to be amazing with or without me. I just hope when I come back you'll want to be amazing with me. I'm so sorry I couldn't be the one to catch you this time, Katie Grace. Next time I'll be a better man and I'll never let you fall again.

My phone vibrates in my hand, shaking me from my memory of the night before. It's a text from Jessica.

She didn't get your message I did. I deleted it. She's not well but she will be eventually. We just got home from the hospital. As if you care. You really should come see her, you'll regret it if you don't. But don't come see her if you're not going to stay, if you can't be with her. I'll be her family and I'll help her with things if you can't. But you should

Michael, you have no clue, but you should. I'm deleting your number because I don't ever want to have to lie to her about knowing how to contact you. For the record I knew you lied about Riley. You loved Katie too much to do that. I know you Michael, better than you know yourself. Don't text me back I can't chance it. Just come back to us.

Shit, damn, fuck! On the one hand I'm relieved she didn't hear the message and on the other hand now she'll never know I tried. Maybe it's best this way. *Why was she in the hospital, though?* Jessica would have said if it was bad. She said she would be okay eventually. *What does eventually mean? Am I ready to go back? Can I tell her everything I've done?* No, not if she's sick or unstable; I couldn't do that to her. I could make her worse not better. I need to give her space. *I* need space.

God please forgive me and somehow make her know that I love her. I love her so much. It's just not our time right now and I can't go back until it is.

Chapter 10 ~ Misty

"So tell me about this girl you've been seeing. For the record, you look happier than I've ever seen you." Daniel passes me a beer and leans up against the counter.

"I'm not seeing anyone; she's a friend, that's all."

"A friend with benefits?"

"Hell no. Just a regular friend."

"I like it. I've known you almost two years now and I've never seen you talk to anyone other than us. Never seen you go hang out with anyone other than us or the guys at work, either. Whatever she's doing to you, let her keep doing it. We're all finally getting a glimpse of happy Mike."

I throw my crumpled up label at him. "So you're saying I've been a miserable prick the entire time you've known me?"

He nods to the table, motioning for us to sit down. "No, not exactly. I just don't think you've really let yourself go and be happy. You're walking around with some pretty heavy demons. I've never asked you about them since that first night we met and I'm not about to now. We all go through some shit and you've gone through yours the past few years. I can't say I'm not curious about your past. I know when you're ready you'll tell me what you want me to know. I consider you my brother, Mike, you know that, right?"

I nod at him, absorbing everything he's saying.

"Good. Talk to me then. Tell me about Misty and what it is about her that makes you so happy that you actually smile now."

"You're an ass, you know that, right? I'm not asking you about your friends."

"Of course I do. Ask away, but you know all of my friends. You, on the other hand, are an anti-social son of a bitch, so I want to know the deal. What is it about this girl that has you acting like what I assume is your normal self?"

He's right. I *have* felt a lot more like my normal self. I'd even cut back on sex. I've even been wondering if it's time to contact the girls. When I put too much thought into it my temper flares and I push the thoughts away. I remember the past and get angry about my dad and about how I acted. I'm not angry at Katherine anymore; I don't think I have been in a long time. After I grab us a couple more beers, I sit back down.

"There's nothing exactly special about her, she's just nice and easy to talk to. Misty reminds me of some people I used to know before my life was turned upside down. Things were simpler then, less complicated. Now that I'm settled in my own place, growing in my position with the company and not partying as much, I guess I'm relaxing a bit. I'm not worried about bumping into my old friends at parties or worried that they're going to track me down and find me anymore. Life is good for a change. You're right, I feel more like my old self. I'm still not ready to go back and mend fences. I'm just not there yet, but I *am* ready to move forward."

Daniel's picking at his label, deep in thought. "You were worried about people tracking you down?"

I nod, "Look, I had the same group of friends from the time I was in elementary school until after high school. We were close, *really* close. Imagine Connor dropping out of your life one day. That's essentially what I did. I'm sure I would have tracked them down if the situation were reversed. I told them not to try and find me, though, and I meant it. So far, so good."

"Fair enough. So are you bringing Misty to our graduation party tomorrow?"

Thank God, change of topic.

"Yeah, she's really excited to meet everyone. You'll like her, she's cute and sweet. She's the kind of girl that genuinely cares about her friends."

Daniel raises an eyebrow at me.

"What?"

"Are you *sure* you don't have feelings for her? Or better yet, are you sure *she* doesn't have feelings for *you*?"

"No, I don't think she does. We're just friends, Daniel. I'm not looking for a relationship. I don't know if I will *ever* be looking for a relationship. My last one was pretty fucking perfect, until it wasn't anymore. I've been pretty forward with her; she knows I'm not looking for a relationship. She's nice and laid back. It's simple and uncomplicated. It's just nice to be around someone of the opposite sex that isn't trying to get me to fuck her."

"Alright, if you say so. Just keep in mind that when a girl is spending a lot of time with a guy, texts him often, and wants to meet his friends, it's usually because she wants *more*. They get that 'I can change his mind' complex and think they'll be the one to turn you into relationship material. Just watch yourself."

"Thanks for your concern, but I've got this under control." *Famous last words.*

~~~***~~~

Daniels words weighed heavily on my mind last night and all day today. I've almost cancelled on Misty at least ten times. I don't want to lead her on. She's the one girl that I could imagine letting myself fall for if my heart wasn't already taken. I couldn't be more obvious of my non-feelings for her and she's never pushed the topic. There's never been any inappropriate touching, or even sexual innuendos between us, so I let it go. Besides, it's my dad's birthday weekend and it always puts me on edge. It will be nice to just have a friendly face around.

Daniel must be in charge of the music because he's a huge Easy E fan and *Boyz in the Hood* is blaring with the bass kicked up high. Misty grabs my hand and I pull her through the crowd, leading her out to the yard where I know they're all waiting.

Introductions are made all around and Connor seems to really like Misty, he even kisses her on the cheek. It doesn't bother me as long as she doesn't hate me after he leads her along for a few weeks and then tells her it won't work out with them. That's Connor's way—he doesn't commit, either. I've never asked why; it isn't my business. I don't think Misty is that into him, though, because she's back at my side pretty quickly. April hands us some drinks and talks with Misty. April can be friends with anyone, effortlessly. She's going to be a great social worker.

Jake passes shots of tequila around to us all. April and Misty took off to the bathroom and Jake huddles the rest of us together.

"I got it today. I think she's going to love it."

Connor pats him on the shoulder. "You're assuming she's going to say yes. It might be in that moment she realizes I'm really the better brother."

Jake punches him in the arm. "Fuck you, Connor. Go find one of your own. April's mine and I can't wait for her to finally wear a real ring instead of that promise ring. I'm tired of watching guys eye fuck her all the time. She has no clue how desirable she is."

"I hate to break it to you, Jake, but a ring isn't going to stop dudes from eye fucking her. In fact, it might bring out a whole different kind of douche pool. The ones that like to fuck taken girls."

Daniel steps between them and changes the subject. *Thank god.* Connor and Jake can get into some nasty fights, *especially* when they're drinking.

"So we're still on for Vegas this weekend, right? Guys trip to celebrate graduation? It's going to be epic. Booze, strip clubs, gambling…sex. Don't worry, Jake, we'll take a rotation so you don't have to be alone."

Jake's lip curls up at the thought, "Daniel, I'm not you. I don't need to have someone hold my hand while I'm alone. You guys can fuck anyone you want, I'll be at the roulette table."

I'm not sure how many shots we've taken by the time the girls get back, but it's a lot because the bottle is empty. My mood has gone downhill fast; I can't stop thinking about my dad. We used to spend his birthdays out on the boat. All of us, even Joseph, would take the time off. Those were some of the best weekends of our lives. Joseph even paid attention to Katherine and she was so happy she glowed. Although she would never admit how happy it made her. *No, not happening, not tonight.*

"Mike, are you okay? You look a little lost in thought."

Misty is smiling up at me. *God, she really is a beautiful thing.* Her cheeks are flushed from the alcohol and she must be hot because she took off her sweater and is walking around in a skin tight V-neck that clings to her tits.

"I'm fine, just thinking about things I shouldn't be. Are you having fun?"

"I am. I like your friends, they're fun. I think I've had too much to drink, though. Can we go over there and sit for a little bit?"

She's pointing to Daniel's garden. I hate to be alone with her over there. She looks so fuckable that I don't trust myself, but I can't tell her no. I don't ever want to tell her no. I want to make her happy; I'm tired of making the girls close to me hate me.

"Sure, let's go."

If I could describe the variety of looks my friends shoot my way, I would say they vary from 'asshole' to 'you lucky son of a bitch go get her.' It's not about that with Misty, though. It can't be.

We sit on the swing for a little bit in silence, looking up at the stars. I try to avoid stargazing at all costs because of the memories it triggers. I wish I had a cure for wiping them away since I can't seem to get the balls to go back to her. Misty laces her fingers in mine and I'm not sure what to do so I don't do anything.

The next thing I know, she's straddling my lap with her arms wrapped around my neck and her mouth on mine. The heat between her legs radiates straight through to my dick which responds faster than my mind can catch up. The kiss is slow and sweet and alarm bells go off in my head. I pull her hands away and hold them behind her back. After biting down hard on her lip, I work my way down her neck.

"Oh god! Mike, yes!"

This is wrong, it is so wrong. I can't do this to her, I care about her enough to stop. I'm not the guy for her, she deserves so much better than me.

"Misty, stop, we can't do this. I'm sorry but it just doesn't feel right."

She looks up at me with desire flaming through her eyes.

"It feels right to me. Stop over thinking this, Mike, and just *feel* it. I feel your dick pressed against me and I know you really don't want to stop."

"If we're going to do this, Misty, we do it *my* way. I don't do sweet and romantic. I fuck, HARD. I bite, HARD. I spank, HARD. And I'll make you come again and again, HARD. But I can't promise tomorrow. At all."

Her big hazel eyes are glossed over from the alcohol and I know this is a bad idea, but she's a big girl and if she thinks she can handle it, who am I to judge her decisions? I was honest with her. I just hope Daniel is wrong and she doesn't think she can change me.

"We're friends, right? We'll be friends tomorrow still and we'll figure it all out later. I want to be with you tonight, Mike. Everything else will fall into place." She flashes me a smile that would melt the hardest of hearts and I feel a slight tug on mine.

Fuck, this is such a bad idea.

~~~***~~~

Long after Misty is asleep, I creep downstairs to sleep on the couch. Connor's good at getting people out of his house after a party. I didn't expect Daniel to be still awake watching TV, though. He looks mad or maybe disappointed.

"Hey."

He nods but doesn't say anything. I walk into the kitchen and grab a bottle of water then come back and sit next to him.

"You have no clue how much that girl likes you, do you? Her eyes were on you all night, Mike. She absolutely adores you. I thought maybe, just maybe, she might be the one to bring you out of this. But the fact that you're down here with me, instead of up there with her, proves how wrong I was. When is it going to be enough for you? Do yourself a favor, Mike. Figure your shit out, because if you're going to open yourself up to friendships you're going to have to draw a line in the sand. Friends or sex, you can't have both. Until you finally get past all the stuff that's holding you down, it won't get any better."

He's right. I don't even know what to say. I royally fucked up tonight. I can't even face what I did. I have no clue how I'm going to face Misty in the morning.

"I know. It was wrong and I have no excuse. It started to get real and I couldn't deal. I'm not ready. I'm an asshole."

"I'm not going to argue with you there. Do her a favor, get her some water and take it upstairs. Don't let her know you're down here avoiding her. Whatever you do tomorrow, that's on you, but don't abandon that girl tonight. She isn't one of your conquests. She just did what all girls do and thought she could fix what's broken inside of you. It happens to the best of us."

It sounds like he's speaking from experience but I don't dare ask. I follow his advice, though, because it's the only thing tonight that has made the slightest bit of sense.

"Thanks, Daniel."

"Anytime, Mike. I've always got your back, brother, no matter what."

Part Three

The Best Things Become a
Triangle

I think reality is starting to sink in a little more as dawn approaches and these memories wash over me like a cold shower. I've spent the past few years being a self-absorbed man whore, never looking past the here and the now.

I've been given the best friends possible and I'm teetering on the brink of destroying each one of them. Is it worth it? In the end, we're all going to be hurt in one way or another. You can't mix this many lives together, this many loves, and have everyone escape unscathed. It's just not possible.

Do I value my friendship with Daniel enough to let go of Kate? Does he value his friendship with me enough to let her come back to me? How am I even involved in a love triangle with my best friend? This is something that should have never happened and I only have myself to blame.

There are only two things in this world I value more than my friendship with Daniel. Kate and Jess. I thought the Vanessa situation was bad, but this is so much worse.

As I lie here and continue down memory lane, there's one thing that is constant in my mind. I've got a chance to get Kate back and I don't care what the end result is as long as that's the outcome. I'm not ready to give up my friends, but if it gets my life back on track with the woman who owns me mind, body and soul, it's a pretty fair trade. Isn't it?

Chapter 11 ~ And Then There Were Four

"What in the hell do you need all those pickles for, Daniel?"

He laughs as he pours what has to be the tenth giant jar into a huge tub. "Aimee and Julie are doing some sorority thing tonight. They can explain it better than I can. It's like bobbing for apples but with pickles. They're calling it 'Pickle Pimping' and I'm sure it will be the highlight of the night. Julie was very specific that no 'little' pickles are allowed."

Looking down into the tub, I see he's right about that. All the pickles are huge, like the ones they sell individually at liquor stores. *Explains why the jars are so big.* I can imagine the sexual thoughts and gestures that will ensue tonight. It could be lots of fun.

"Okay, so I get the pickles I guess, but what's with the pile of sombreros over there?"

He just shrugs his shoulders. "I'm not exactly sure, but we'll find out. Aimee just said they needed enough sombreros for every guy coming tonight to have one."

"Pickle pimping women and sombrero wearing men. Ladies and gentlemen, the theme of the evening, come one, come all to the greatest sombrero laden, pickle pimping orgy around. Fuck, dude, this could get really interesting. I'm game, but I've got dibs on the best pickle pimper. Well, as long as she's hot and *not* a repeat."

He laughs and just shakes his head. "I don't know, Mike, I think Julie could win that one and since you've already had her, you might have to settle for a few down the line."

Holy shit! This mother fucker knows that Julie could win which can only mean one thing.

"When?"

He looks up at me, confused. "When what?"

I'm staring him down big time, but I really don't think he realizes he just slipped up. *This is going to be fun. He never talks about this kind of stuff.* "*When* did you fall into the threesome with Julie and Aimee?"

His cheeks flush and he tries to back pedal, "Don't even bother denying it, Daniel, you *just* said Julie could win. You would only know the depth of skill that woman has with a dick in her mouth if you've been there. Why the hell didn't you say anything? I'll tell you, there are still days where I wish I could go back to them and have a do over. I know a hell of a lot more now than I did then."

Daniel taps the keg, fills up a couple beers, and leans against it, passing a beer to me. "Alright, I don't want to be a bitch and make you pinky swear or anything, but I just don't want anyone knowing this. *Especially* Connor…he gossips like a little girl."

"Understandable, some things are shared between certain brothers and not others. You've got my word."

"It was last weekend. Connor and Jake were up at their parents' and you were up north at that job site. I came down for the weekend while my house was being fumigated. Julie and Aimee came over to watch movies, nothing out of the ordinary. We started playing truth or dare which really turned into a whole lotta shots with whatever truths or dares were asked. I found out that their biggest fantasy is for you and me to team up with them for some fun. By then, we were all pretty drunk. I told them I could see the logic in that so they could both be satisfied at the same time. Julie pounced and said she can't have a foursome with someone that they haven't had a threesome with yet. At the time, that made complete and total sense to me. Anyway, I'm not going to go into details, but I will say that my mind was blown and that was the hottest sex of my life."

Once I finish choking on my beer over the foursome comment I can respond, "They are something, aren't they? I mean, just the way Julie can get Aimee to come by sucking on her clit and the sounds they make. Fuck. It's so hot."

A slow smile spread across his face and I know he's replaying that in his head. I replay it all the time and probably always will.

"So, what did you tell them about the foursome?"

"Dude, do you even have to ask?"

"Well, with a normal guy, no. But, Daniel, my man, you are *far* from normal. It took you how many years to finally go for it? I'm game if you are. I don't care if you watch me fuck as long as we're not fucking each other."

I watch as his gaze trails over my shoulder and a huge smile appears on his face. Suddenly, I'm flanked by the girls, one on each side, each kissing me hello on the cheek.

"So Mike, Daniel and Aimee and I were talking the other night."

I'm not going to let them know he told me. I want to hear them ask for it. "Oh yeah? What about?"

They glance at Daniel, but he just shrugs his shoulders. He knows my game and I can tell by the way his eyes are all lit up and shit, that he's down for it, too. Our night just got a whole lot more interesting.

Aimee steps in front of me, wrapping her arms around my neck and pulling me down so close that my lips are just a whisper away from hers. "Mike, we want you *and* Daniel in our bed tonight. We want to feel you both, *experience* you both at the same time."

Her lips brush against mine, her tongue gliding across my top lip as I open to give her access. I easily pick her up, she wraps her legs around my waist, and I back her up against the tree next to me. I take control of the kiss, biting her lip and grinding against her so she feels how hard my dick is.

"I'm game, but this time I know some new tricks, and if we do this, we do it *my* way. This time the men are in control. If you can get Julie to agree to that, I'll take you places you've never been before, sunshine."

Her heart is racing against my chest but a smirk flashes across her face. "Your wish is *our* command…Sir."

Now, we're getting somewhere. Fuck me. With a quick glance over my shoulder, Daniel has Julie in a similar position. *This is going to be an interesting night.*

I gently place Aimee back on the ground as Julie and Daniel come over to us. "Okay, boys, you know we usually don't care who knows who we fuck. However, tonight is a fantasy fulfillment, so if you don't mind can we just keep this between us? When you guys are ready, just head over to our house, but don't come too late. We want to experience this fantasy to the hilt."

Daniel exhales a sigh of relief. I know he doesn't want anyone to know about last time, so he *really* doesn't want anyone to know about this.

"Of course, you have our word. Just remember my stipulation, ladies. We're in control tonight, not the other way around."

Julie shoots Aimee a 'what the fuck' look but Aimee just smiles sweetly at her and pulls her into a very slow and passionate kiss. I'm somewhat envious of them. They're so in love and yet so willing to explore their sexual desires with other people together, without any jealousy. I would have never been able to handle something like that. Just seeing Katherine talk to another guy, especially Marc, used to set me off. I never thought being possessive was a bad thing, but looking at these two, I wonder what side of love possession falls on. The good side or the bad?

~~~***~~~

If you would have told me when I got here tonight that not only would I be turned on watching girls 'pimp pickles' from a tub, but also realize that I'd fantasize over it for a long time to come, I would've told you that you were crazy. Watching these girls lick, bite, and suck those giant pickles into their mouths is so fucking erotic.

There's a cute little blonde that's been trying to get my attention all night. I would almost say she's shy, but honestly, she rubs me the wrong way. Calculated would be the word used to describe her. I won't lie though, the way she locked eyes with me while she was sucking that pickle into her mouth had my dick perking up a bit.

And did I forget to mention that the sombreros were our outfits for the night? Yeah, every guy in this place is wearing nothing but his underwear and a sombrero. They were even prepared with extra boxers in a variety of sizes for those who showed up commando. What's hilarious is that you can tell which guys are aroused. More than a handful are covering their junk with their sombrero. Hell, I don't give a fuck *who* sees my dick at attention. I could hang that mother fucking sombrero off the tip of my dick like a hat rack. Some of these other guys probably aren't as lucky.

"Damn, Mike, that blonde girl has been eyeing you up all night. Are you going to hit that or what?"

"Nah, Connor, that girl gives me some serious bad vibes. I'm not sure what it is about her, but I'm not going anywhere near her."

"Dude, you're trippin', but I'm going to hail to the pussy master and back the fuck off that one. You typically have a sense about those girls that bring trouble and I don't want to be stuck in a shithole again."

I'm laughing so hard I'm about to lose my sombrero. Daniel is heading our way and it's almost time to make our exit. The earlier we leave, the more fun we get to have.

"What's so funny?" Daniel asks as he pours himself a beer.

"Connor seems to think I've got some interesting skills."

"It's true! You're a mother fucking pussy master! No joke, it's like you're one of those snake charmers. You just flash a look and girls are all over your jock. Don't get me wrong, I get my share, but I have to work for it."

"He's right. There *is* something about you that brings the girls running."

"Okay, first of all, you don't *have* to work for it, Connor, you *choose* to work for it. Even if you don't realize it, that's what you're doing. You could have any of these girls, anytime, but you feel like you have some reputation to uphold so you throw parties and entice the girls further.

You're rich, and you're not ugly, but even if you were, rich trumps ugly. Stop being such a pleaser and you won't have to work for it. Truth is, my man, you *like* working for it. It's part of the game for you, and that's cool. Whatever gets your dick wet. Secondly, if you haven't noticed, I've *never* approached a girl. I've *never* initiated a conversation. I'm *always* indifferent. I'm not looking for anything other than a random hook-up. Girls have that radar, they either want to fix me or know they can get their dirtiest fantasies fulfilled by me because I'm indifferent. It's what gets *my* dick wet. Call it what you want, I'll be the pussy master if you want me to. At the end of the day, I'm just looking to stay away from drama. I've had enough of that to last me a lifetime."

Speaking of drama, the cute little blonde has finally worked her way over here. She's hot up close—curves in all the right places, nice tits, tight ass—but I still can't shake my gut feeling on this one. Daniel, on the other hand, seems to be very interested. She introduces herself as Vanessa, and even though she's friendly with us all, she's flirting with me. I'm not interested. Eventually, she gets the hint and starts putting her attention into Daniel. Poor guy is falling for it hook, line, and sinker. He's so into her he doesn't even notice she's still giving me looks. Connor took off already and I really want to get next door to the girls. I'm hoping to get Daniel out of here unscathed.

"Daniel, we gotta go take care of those favors we promised the neighbors."

A quick flash of excitement shows in Daniel's eyes. *Thank god, at least he isn't completely lost to this girl yet. I'm going to have to talk to him about her.*

"You're right, I completely lost track of time. It was so nice meeting you, Vanessa. I hope we'll see you again soon."

She flashes him the world's biggest smile, "I would love that. Here, what's your cell number? I'll call you so you can save my number. We should definitely get together again soon."

After they exchange numbers she hugs Daniel goodbye. His back is to me but she looks right at me, licks her lips, and mouths 'later Mike' to me. I knew she was flirting, but she has some serious issues if she's flirting with me behind his back like that. I don't want to wreck his mood tonight but decide to have a talk with him about it later.

Chapter 12 ~ The Devil Wears Louboutins

"Connor, you know on any given day I would be at your party in a heartbeat but I just can't be around Vanessa. I've tried so hard to make her understand I don't want anything to do with her and she's still flirting with me. Making inappropriate comments to me behind Daniel's back. It sucks donkey balls being in the middle of this shit."

He exhales loudly before speaking, "I know, Mike, and I get where you're coming from, I do. I can't stand that vicious bitch, either. I need you to be my wingman tonight. We're going to get one over on Vanessa. I met this girl, her name is Debbie and I swear, Mike, she is the spitting image of Vanessa. I told her I have a friend I want her to meet tonight so you have to come."

I groan and shake my head, knowing he can't see me.

"Come on, Mike! I know it's not your thing to be set up, but this is going to make Vanessa lose her shit. Think about it, you won't be with her, won't even give her the time of day and yet here you are with a girl that could be her identical twin. She's going to breathe fire she'll be so pissed, and maybe Daniel will *finally* see her for what she really is. A money grubbing, dick sucking, friend fucking twat."

"Hey, she hasn't fucked me yet so please don't group me into her nastiness."

"Yeah, not yet, but she would if she could."

I take a deep breath and let it out slowly. He's right and this *could* be a way to make Daniel finally see her for what she really is.

"Okay, fine, I just hope this Debbie girl isn't as crazy as her twin."

~~~***~~~

On the way to Connor's, all I can think about is the night we met Vanessa. If I would have just spoken up then and told Daniel what I thought of her we wouldn't be in this mess. Instead, I waited until the next day. After our absolutely exhausting and unforgettable night with Aimee and Julie, we passed out. When the girls and I woke up, Daniel was long gone. I found out after checking my texts that he was so excited and felt such a connection with Vanessa, he woke up in the morning and took her out for breakfast. I didn't see him again until late that night. Unfortunately, by then he was really crushing on her and as he told me about their day I just didn't have the heart to tell him my suspicions or what she did. I've regretted that choice every single day since.

Vanessa treats Daniel like shit. I'm pretty sure she's only with him because he's rich. She's always getting him to buy her expensive shoes. I know he's got the money but that isn't the point. Vanessa is demanding and condescending to everyone, even him at times. Yet every once in a while, when she thinks she's alone with him, you can almost believe she's human and really cares for him. If she wasn't constantly hitting on me and trying to get in my pants I would almost believe she loves him. *Almost.*

Vanessa has put a damper on everything. No one likes her. Even sweet April can't stand her. If April can't find something to like about you, there is *definitely* something wrong with you. I've got a bad feeling about tonight. I wish I had *never* agreed to come. There was traffic, so now I'm late and Connor called already to tell me Debbie is there and waiting. I was hoping I would get there in time to have a few drinks, loosen up, and relax before meeting her. Now I'm stuck having to go in with my game face on. *I just hope we know what we're doing.* Thankfully, Daniel and Vanessa left after I did. Vanessa needed new shoes; she couldn't *possibly* wear the same pair she had on at the last party. I really wish Daniel would put her in check. I know he's getting fed up. I saw the look on his face when he paid off his last credit card bill; he wasn't happy. Even so, he's a class act. He's never said a bad thing about her. I guess that's what happens when you're head over heels in love. It's just sad it had to be Vanessa to take his heart. He deserves a girl like April or Katherine.

I've been thinking more about her lately, and about Jessica. I miss them. I think they would fall into my new life seamlessly and easily make friends with mine. I know I'm getting closer to trying to make amends. I'm just not there yet. I'm not ready to explain what I've done and I'd *have* to explain. I'm sure they're happier without me in their lives anyway.

~~~***~~~

When I walk in the house, I'm immediately greeted by April. She's been assigned lookout duty because she's waiting for me with three shots of tequila. I pound them all in a row as my body absorbs not only the alcohol, but the massive amounts of bass shooting through me while *Straight Outta Compton* by Dr. Dre pumps through the surround sound speakers.

After the shots April gives me a big hug.

"What's with the welcome wagon?"

She flicks me in the head. "What, can't a girl be nice?"

"Of course, and you're one of the nicest, but you usually don't meet me at the door with shots."

"Busted. I just wanted you to loosen up a bit. I know Connor roped you in to doing this. But damn, Mike, Debbie *does* look a lot like Vanessa. I'm talking double take. And although I can appreciate the girl's beauty, I know it might be hard for you to get past seeing bitchface when you look at her. I thought the shots would help you out a bit."

I give her a quick peck on the cheek, "And that is why you're one of the best women I know. Thanks for looking out but I'll be fine. Just a few hours and I'll go pass out."

"You know, Mike, in all the years I've known you, you've never said anything about your past. I'm curious to know who the other best women you know are. Maybe you can fill me in someday?"

Leave it to a woman to take an opening and run with it. She's probably been waiting for an opening like that for a long time. "Sure, April, not anytime soon but someday I'll tell you all about them. If I get lucky, I might even be able to introduce you someday. But for today, lead me to the torture chamber."

She giggles at me and I can tell she's been drinking because April is *so* not a giggler. "Your wish is my command."

As we cross through the living room, I see Connor in the kitchen with a girl. The closer we get I almost start to wonder how Daniel and Vanessa beat me here. That's how much Debbie looks like Vanessa. Sure there are subtle differences, but you know how they say everyone has a twin? Well, Debbie, without a doubt, is Vanessa's.

"Mike, it's about time! Come meet Debbie. Debbie, this is my friend, Mike." The look in Connor's eyes is purely devious; he can't wait for Vanessa to lose her lid.

I made nice with Debbie for about an hour before Daniel and Vanessa arrived. We were all around the fire pit when they got there and the look on Vanessa's face was beyond priceless. Daniel seemed a little taken aback, too, but he recovered nicely. Connor made introductions and they pulled up some chairs and joined us. Vanessa quickly ditched her chair and crawled up into Daniel's lap instead. I don't know how he does it; just *looking* at her makes my skin crawl. After bragging to everyone about the new pair of

Louboutins Daniel bought her, she finally decided to ask questions.

"So, where did you meet Debbie? It's crazy how much we look like each other! I didn't realize you had a thing for blondes, Mike."

"Connor introduced us tonight; he thought we might hit it off. I've never limited myself to hair color, Vanessa. I pick my women based on their personalities and our sexual chemistry. Nothing more, nothing less."

Smart girl that she is, Debbie picks up on the tension immediately, hopefully Daniel does, too. "It *is* interesting how much we look alike, but it's California and I guess us blondes are a dime a dozen here."

That earns Debbie a few laughs and takes her up a couple notches in my book. She isn't going to let Vanessa get to her, either. She leans over and whispers in my ear, "I'm not sure what the game is here, but I *don't* like her so I'm up for it. This could be fun. I'll follow your lead if you want to play."

This girl is awesome and I most definitely want to play. This is going to be so much fun. Leaning into her, I take the lead and pull her into a quick kiss. She's actually very responsive, and I wonder if she'll stick around for some fun later.

"I'll be back in a few. I'm going to hit the head and I'll bring another bottle of tequila out when I come back. Play nicely while I'm gone."

When I step out of the bathroom, I'm shocked to see Vanessa sitting on the bed. There was a line downstairs but I knew there wouldn't be one upstairs.

"What in the hell kind of game are you playing, Mike?"

She's pissed.

"I don't know what you're talking about. I'm not playing any games."

"Oh come off it! You just happen to be here tonight with a girl that looks like me? Is this your subtle way of telling me you want me after all? I'm ready and willing, Mike, whenever you are. I've wanted you since the moment I laid eyes on you."

While she's talking, she has gotten so close to me that I'm essentially backed into a wall, trying to get as far away from her as possible. Her fingers caress my face and it gives me the chills. *She's a crazy bitch!* My temper flares and I push her hand off of my face.

"You have a boyfriend, Vanessa, what about him? Daniel loves you and you would just throw that away to have sex with me? Even if I *did* want you, which I don't, you would be willing to give up Daniel for a one night stand?"

"I like Daniel. He's kind and gentle and he gives me whatever I want, whenever I want it. He's great and I *could* make it work with him but I would rather make it work with you instead. Can't you feel the sexual heat between us, Mike? It's so intense. Just looking at you and hearing your voice makes me almost come in my panties. Here, feel for yourself." She pulls my hand and tries to get me to feel under her dress. That's when I lose my shit.

"You have no idea how men work, do you? Do you think that men, and I'm talking *real* men, Vanessa, not these boys you must be used to messing with. Do you think that men do this kind of shit to each other? Sleep with their best friend, their freaking brother's girl? They don't. Real men have each other's backs. This shit ends tonight, you got it? It's over. I'm telling him everything you've done up until now and I'm telling him about tonight."

"He won't believe you."

I was heading toward the door but the chill in her tone has the hair on my neck standing up.

"He has no reason not to."

The smile that flashes across her face is one of victory. It's got my stomach in knots. *What did she do?*

"I get what I want, Mike. *Always*. I've been telling Daniel for months that I think you're flirting with me, hitting on me. I told him I'm uncomfortable around you. Why do you think when we're all together he pulls me close, marks his territory, and shows me so much affection? It's because I've planted the seed. That's all it takes, he can dismiss it and say he doesn't believe it, but at the end of the day he will. It's my word against yours. We've been gone a while. I've been in line for the bathroom but what's your excuse?"

Damn. I've got no choice but to call her bluff and hope that Connor, Jake and April will have my back.

"Do what you have to, Vanessa, I'm over this. Just be warned, if you tell him your days are numbered, but then again they're numbered even if you don't tell him."

On the way downstairs I get sidetracked in the kitchen by some girls who decided they wanted to bake some cookies. They were pretty baked themselves and I convinced one of Connor's friends to run to the store and get them some cookies instead. By the time I got back outside they had already brought the tequila out and started the shots without me. It makes me so sick seeing Vanessa there all cuddly in Daniel's arms and he has no clue what a deceptive bitch she really is. As much as he deserves to know, I'm dreading the fact that I have to be the one to break his heart.

~~~***~~~

When I wake up in the morning I've got a pounding headache. I'm in the guest room and can't remember how I got here. The last thing I remember is coming outside after the bathroom and taking a couple of shots. Vanessa kept smirking at me and it was really pissing me off so I tried passing the time by making out with Debbie. I vaguely remember sex because she kept telling me to yell her name. I don't usually do that, I usually have control. I keep trying to remember the details, but after that my memory is an absolute blank.

Getting out of bed kills me. I ache everywhere. *What the hell happened last night? Why can't I remember anything?* I've been drunk as hell before but never blackout drunk. Maybe I'll feel better after some coffee and some ibuprofen. The house is super quiet as I drag myself down the stairs, feeling every aching muscle as I go. I could be getting sick. That would explain the aches, and since I don't get sick often, when I do it's pretty bad.

Thankfully, somebody's awake because the smell of coffee meets me head on. I'm eternally grateful for not having to wait for a pot to brew. Since I have no clue what time it is, they could all be up and out of the house by now. It would also explain why it's so quiet. As I make my way into the kitchen, I'm shocked to see that they're all sitting at the table. Quite honestly, they look like someone died. *This is not good.*

"Morning, guys" I barely croak out, even my voice doesn't want to work today.

"Morning, Mike" they all reply in unison. *Odd. Daniel's head is in his hands and he isn't making eye contact with anyone. I hope he's okay.*

"So how was your night last night, Mike? Did you and Debbie hit it off?" Well, at least Connor seems normal.

"I guess so. Honestly, guys, I don't remember much after coming back from the bathroom and taking those first two shots. Everything after that is missing. I think I sort of remember she had a fetish about me calling out her name over and over. I don't think I've ever said Debbie so much in my life. Other than that, it's all a blank. I'm tired, my body hurts, and my head is pounding. If I didn't know any better, I would think someone slipped me a roofie."

They all exchange an odd look with each other like maybe somebody *did* slip me a roofie. Daniel finally lifts his head and he looks like hell. It looks like he hasn't slept at all. *What in the world is going on around here? I'm thinking I missed something major last night.*

"Guys, I'm getting a really bad vibe here. Can someone please tell me what I'm missing?

"Yeah, Mike, I can. Come in the other room and we'll talk, just the two of us."

I follow Daniel's lead into the living room, coffee in hand, and take a seat on the couch. April brings me a couple of ibuprofen and gives me a kiss on the cheek, whispering in my ear "It will be okay, we all love you" before she walks away. That was ominous and suddenly my heart is racing. *Did something happen to Katherine?* I quickly calm myself down because even if something had, they would have no clue about that.

"Daniel, can you tell me what the hell happened last night?" Daniel is sitting on the table in front of me, anger flashing though his eyes, but it's more than that—he's hurt. *Oh man, Vanessa must have told him her lies. That would explain his mood.*

"I don't know how to say this so I'm just going to come out with it. You slept with Vanessa last night."

His words aren't angry as he says them, just very sad. I feel like I've been sucker punched in the gut. That just isn't possible. I would never, *ever* do that to him.

"No...no, I didn't. I was... Debbie and I...we hit it off. Why would you say that? I would *never* do that to you, Daniel. You're my brother, she's your girl. Shit, I can't stand the bitch I wouldn't DO THAT!"

I close my eyes and wrack my brain, willing memories I don't have to come. I can't even picture her with me in the room. I don't even know if I really fucked her, I just remember calling her name over and over. I wouldn't have done that unless I had been having sex with her, though, otherwise that would have been weird.

When I open my eyes again, Daniel's crying and I know that even if I don't remember last night I have somehow irrevocably changed our friendship. He and his family brought me into their world and loved me when I had *nothing* and I repaid him like this. *I'm such a piece of shit.*

"Daniel, I'm so sorry, man." I'm crying just as much as he is and choking over my words. "I never meant to hurt you. I would never. I'm just so fucking sorry. I'll go grab my stuff and get out of here. I'll head over to see your old man and resign. I don't want you to have to be reminded of this at work."

Suddenly, I'm wrapped in his arms. We're hugging and crying, and normally it would be a little uncomfortable, but at this moment it's what we both need. I haven't cried like this since my dad died. I'm just so unbelievably sorry.

"You're not going anywhere, Mike. We're going to figure this out. I know you wouldn't do this to me. Brothers over bitches, right?"

"Right. But god, man, I'm just so sorry. I don't even know…"

"I know, so let's piece it together. Tell me everything that happened last night. Start from the beginning."

So I do, but I start from the night we met Vanessa. I tell him everything. When I get to the part about what she said to me last night I can see his heart breaking even more. Even though I didn't do it on purpose, I still feel an incredible amount of guilt. He loves her so much.

"You know she's not like that when we're together. That's what doesn't make any sense. Yes, she has her moments where she's demanding, but when it's just the two of us, she's sweet and caring. I just don't get it."

"I don't know what to tell you, I really don't. Connor's seen her in action so you can confirm it with him if you need to. I don't blame you for not trusting me right now."

"It's true!" Connor yells from the kitchen, causing us both to laugh. I guess we forgot they were in there. The rooms aren't exactly far apart and they've been listening the whole time, I'm sure of it.

"Daniel, I need you to fill in the pieces of last night that I don't remember. Maybe it will trigger something."

"Yeah, of course. Hey you guys, come in here and help me fill Mike in. There are pieces I wasn't there for, either."

It's moments like these that make me appreciate everything I have in my life. My amazing friends and their support means more to me than anything. It's also moments like these that make me miss Katherine and Jessica the most. April sits next to me and holds my hand. I think back to the first day I met Jake and how intimidating he was to me. Now, April sitting next to me while she holds my hand doesn't even make him flinch. Jake and I are just as close as Daniel and I are but in different ways. He knows how much I value his relationship with April. He knows I used to have something similar with someone and we talk about it. Well, we talk about it as much as I do with anyone else, which isn't that much. I don't think he feels like he can bounce relationship issues around with Daniel and Connor because they've never been there.

Over the next hour, they fill me in on everything that happened last night. Debbie got really drunk really fast, too. They just thought she wasn't used to drinking so Daniel and Vanessa put her in a cab home. I went upstairs by myself and crashed. Somewhere along the line, Vanessa snuck in and had sex with me, pretending to be Debbie. We can't figure out the end game here. The only thing we can come up with is that she knew she was caught and that I was going to tell Daniel—which I was—and she had sex with me like she'd wanted to from the beginning.

April agrees with me that it seems like she slipped something in my drink and Debbie's.

Vanessa was the one that took the tequila and the glasses outside when I got distracted so it would have been very easy for her to do it. Connor called Debbie and she's fine this morning and she remembers everything, so it seems I'm the only one that was really affected. April wants me to go to the police, but we have no proof. Even if that was it, there were over a hundred people here last night. I could have picked up the wrong drink, although it's doubtful. I'm fine, other than the mess I've caused. Or that *she* caused. What makes me sick is that I'm sure we didn't use a condom. I desperately need to go take a shower and wash that tramp off of me. Daniel and I plan to go STD testing tomorrow and again in six months. This sucks. I've never *not* used a condom except with Katherine and that's how I wanted it to stay. This whole situation gives me the creeps just thinking about it.

"What are you going to do, Daniel? Are you going to call her and confront her?" There's so much compassion in April's eyes when she asks him this question. Their relationship is a lot like mine was with Jessica, but April's a lot calmer than Jessica would be. Jessica would be at Vanessa's house right now giving her a beat down. Just picturing that makes my heart ache for my friend. I miss her.

"No, I'm not. There's no point. She knows what she did. If she has the balls to come try and explain it away I will, but unless that happens, it's over. I sure know how to pick 'em, don't I? I'm sorry, guys. I had no idea she was so conniving. And to think, I almost had myself convinced that she could be the one. "

"Daniel McCormick! Stop it right now. This was not your fault, and it wasn't Mike's fault, either. Vanessa must have some really deep issues to have played the two of you like this. I think it's wise to stay far away from her. Usually, when people do something like this it's because there's a deeper hurt within them that they're trying to run from. It's just unfortunate she found you two to take the brunt of her issues. We'll get past this, just give it some time."

Chapter 13 ~ Fallout

It's been two months since Daniel and Vanessa broke up. I left Connor's house that day with my heavy heart, just hoping things would work out. I thought for sure Daniel would eventually get angry at me and blame me for what happened, but he never did. I don't think I've ever met anyone besides Katherine with a heart and soul as pure as his. Daniel's love for his friends and family runs deep into the core of everything that makes him one of the best people I've ever had the privilege of knowing and loving.

The past few years, Daniel has helped me become a better man. I finally feel like I'm becoming what I wanted all along—a man with a purpose and a life independent from the expectations of others. I'm suddenly on the other side of the fence and wish I could help *him*. Daniel has fallen into a deep pit of loss and heartbreak; I know the feeling well. I don't think he misses Vanessa, that's not what this is about. I think it's more that he gave his heart and soul completely to someone else and she shattered his trust. I know exactly how that feels, and I have absolutely no advice to give him on how to get out of it.

We've tried to get him out of the house to go to the gym, the bar, hell, we even tried a guys' trip to Vegas but he didn't even want to go. For some reason, he's spending all his time in his old room at his parents' house. I figure he's staying there because his house reminds him of all the time he spent there with *her*. Bev is worried and Rick is basking in the glory that he was right about

Vanessa. Even so, he's lightened up a lot on Daniel. For six months he's been a real ass to him because, like me, he got a bad vibe from Vanessa. At least Daniel's still working, but even then he's somewhat distracted which isn't a good thing in the construction business. Rick has been trying to keep him off anything he could really screw up or get hurt doing since his head isn't really in it.

The crazy part of it all is that we've grown closer. I was so afraid he was going to cut me out of his life completely, but it's almost as if our crazy experience has bonded us even more. Vanessa did contact him, and they had it out, but since then she's left him alone. I wish I could say I've been as lucky, but she's called and texted me. I just keep deleting them and ignoring the calls. I hope that she gets the hint soon because I don't want anything to do with her crazy ass.

Since I couldn't get Daniel to come with me, it's just Jake and I hanging out at his house. April's off at a baby shower for a friend of hers.

"So do you think April's going to come back home dreaming of pre-wedding babies?"

Jake snorts, "Hardly. That girl is dead set on establishing not only a career but our marriage before having kids. If it were up to me, we'd already have kids. We've been together almost twelve years now and I'm tired of putting everything on hold. That's weird, right? Most guys would be happy to dodge kids but I'm ready to jump right in."

I think back to how badly I wanted babies with Katherine right after high school. I can only imagine how much that want would have grown if we had stayed together.

"No, I don't think it's weird. You're just being honest. At least she knows how you feel. She knows you're so in love with her that you're ready to take that step. Even if she won't admit it, I'm sure that makes her feel confident in your relationship. Not that she doesn't already, but kids just kind of solidify things. I get where you're coming from even if most guys wouldn't."

He's quiet while he flips the burgers on the grill and drinks his beer. "You know, Mike, I don't pry into your life and never would, but I've pieced together enough over the years to know that whoever she was, you need her."

"Yeah, that might be true, but needing someone and being what's best for them, or them being what's best for you, aren't always the same thing."

"True. I don't know what you were like before but I know you've changed the past few years. She might see those changes and like them. Hell, I'm not one to give relationship advice. By the grace of God I met April in high school and have been lucky enough to hold on to her ever since. She's the only real relationship I've ever had. I can imagine if I didn't have her I would do what you do after a while."

"What is it you think I do?"

He shakes his head and laughs at me. "You know what you do you, fool. You screw anything you can, whenever you can, but you never take one home and you never talk to them again.

You're trying to forget her but it's not working, is it?"

Well, looks like Jake isn't just quietly brooding all the time; he's actually paying attention. I kind of figured, but I never really thought he was putting that much thought into me.

"Look, after that first day when I accused you of checking April out, I also noticed that when you looked at her or us it was with a reverence, or a longing maybe. But it was also with a deep sadness. That's why I eased off of you. I knew you were coming off of something bad, something you missed. I've been hoping that you would have figured it all out by now but I guess not."

"It's complicated."

"The best things in our lives typically are."

"True that. Look, I'm thinking about it, a lot, but I don't know when or if the right time will ever come. Sometimes you just have to leave the past in the past."

"And sometimes you have to stir shit up when it's important. Are your dreams getting better?"

How in the hell does he know about my dreams?

"How do you know about those?"

"That night Vanessa roofied your ass, you went up to crash and we passed you on the way into the house. You were muttering something to the effect of 'hopefully tonight I won't have any more goddamn dreams' and we didn't say anything because it's not our business, but I can piece two and two together pretty well."

I really wish we were not having this conversation right now. "Look, Jake, I appreciate you looking out for me, I do. I hope that you can keep your observations to yourself. I came here for a fresh start and I found it. Other than the nightly dreams that bring my old life crashing into my new one, things are great. I know I'm going to have to get some closure or something eventually because someday I'll want to move on. Until then, let it go."

"Fair enough. I'll let it go and keep it all to myself *if* you answer me one question."

I draw a deep breath and let it out. "Shoot"

"Did you love her like I love April and did she love you back the same?"

"That's *two* questions, asshat."

Jake smirks at me, "Consider it one; I didn't take a breath in between them."

God that sounds like something Connor would say.

"Look, I've watched you guys for a while. You have an effortlessness to your love that we didn't have. I'm not sure why we didn't have that, at the time I thought we did. We had a soul searing, long lasting, and all-encompassing love. When we crashed and burned it was hard, fast, and messy. There were casualties in the destruction, other people got hurt. It wasn't fun. I still can't really talk about it. Just take my advice, hold on to April and don't let her go. If I wasn't such an asshole, I probably could have avoided the entire thing."

Nodding, he replies, "For what it's worth, you're not really an asshole anymore. And for the record, if there's one thing I've learned in my life, it's that the best pieces of ourselves are worth fixing when they break."

I know he isn't referring to me, but to my relationship, and he has a point.

My phone starts ringing and I know it's Vanessa before I even look at it.

Saved by the bell. "Is that her again?"

"Yeah."

"Are you going to tell Daniel she keeps calling you?"

I've asked myself that a dozen times.

"I don't think so. What will that accomplish? It'll either piss him off or make him even sadder. I know she hasn't called him. She'll get the hint eventually; I have nothing to say to her."

We're mostly quiet while we eat our burgers. Jake offers me a beer but I decline, taking water instead. I have to drive back up tonight and I'm going to try like hell to get Daniel out of that room.

"I've noticed you're not really drinking anymore, is it because of that night?"

"Yup, I don't ever want to get myself in that situation again. I like control and I didn't have any that night. I still feel sick about the whole thing."

"I've been wanting to ask you something but didn't know exactly how to. So fuck politically correct, I just want to know. Do you feel like she took advantage of you?"

"No, but I'm disgusted and honestly creeped out by the entire situation. I think from the tiny bit I remember that I must have been into it and I'm sure that was only because I didn't know it was her. It's still hard to reconcile that I wasn't having sex with Debbie. I don't know for sure that Vanessa put anything in my drink so I think that helps me not dwell on it completely. If I had been coherent, I would've never been with Vanessa. She gave me the willies from day one."

"So what's the plan now?"

"I'm going to head back and try to get Daniel out of the house. Do you want to come? It might help."

"Ha! You know that isn't going to help. We've been down this road. He'll come around when he's ready. I'm going to stick around here. April wants to talk wedding stuff when she gets back."

"Well, you have fun with that one. Just agree to it all and you'll be fine."

"Man, isn't that the truth. At least when I'm agreeable she seems to get horny, so it works out in my favor."

"Later, man."

"Later, Mike. Hey, one more thing before you go. If something that bad ever happens to April and me, the way it happened to you, remind me to swallow my pride. I'm good at being stubborn and I don't want to lose out on years with her that I can never get back. Especially when we *all* know she's the one that owns me heart and soul."

Son of a bitch

"Will do, and point well made."

~~~***~~~

Even though I want to get back to Daniel, I detour and take PCH home. There's a beautiful sunset tonight that looks amazing reflected in the ocean. Last month marked three years since the last day I spent with Katherine in our spot. I knew it was inevitable that I would eventually be drawn here, like a moth to the flame, right?

The beach is a very sensory laden place for me. It sets off every sensor in my body. I love the scent of the ocean, and walking barefoot through the sand continuously pulls memories to the front of my mind. They're so overwhelming and difficult to process and yet so comforting at the same time. From the first day I got my license, the beach had become our special place. I wonder if she still comes here. I look around as the thought flickers through my mind, as if she's suddenly going to transport here just because I'm thinking about her. There's no one around, though, just me and my memories.

"Michael, I know the Bahamas were nice but don't you love it so much better here? Someday when we're ready to settle down we should buy that house up there on the bluff. How amazing would it be to live in our favorite place?"

"Hmm, pretty amazing. I don't know, the Bahamas were pretty amazing, too. The water was clear, the beach was private, the drinks were tropical, my sexy as fuck girlfriend was naked, and the sex was off the charts amazing. I don't think either of us have ever let our inhibitions go like we did that day. It was hot, imagine how much hotter it will get as we get older."

"It was pretty hot and a nice end to a crappy trip. I was way too sick the entire vacation. Seeing the island doctor was not my idea of fun."

"Maybe not, but we can have some fun now. How about we let our inhibitions go and take a walk down memory lane. Are you game?"

That was my first missed opportunity—right before I made love to her in the ocean I should have proposed. I wasn't ready to leave our own private paradise and once I proposed I wanted us locked away on the boat, so I waited. *What is it they always say? Hindsight is twenty/twenty, if I knew then what I know now…*

"So are you ready for next week? I'm so freaking excited I can't stand it."

"Nah, I think instead of moving you to the condo I'm going to kidnap you."

"Oh really? And why would you want to do that?"

She was so beautiful, her emerald green bikini showed off all her curves and my baby had amazing curves. I ran my hands across her shoulders and pulled her even closer to me. My lips were just a kiss away from hers.

"Because it's time I have you all to myself. No more sharing you unless it's with our kids. Let's just run away and live in the Bahamas. It could be such a great life. With your money and mine we'd never have to work or go to school. We could just spend our days making love on our private beach."

Before I had a chance to close the small gap between us with a kiss that I would follow up with the big question, she laughed at me.

"Michael, as much as that is an interesting idea, we can't go anywhere. We have school starting and kids are so far into our future they're just speckles of dust in the outer layers of the atmosphere right now. Besides, what about our families and Jessica?"

"Jessica can come with us. We'll find her a nice guy to fall in love with, and until then, she can be our nanny. Who cares about our families? They're rich, they'll come and visit."

"Not that I'm considering this for a second, but Jessica would probably make a really good nanny. With as much shit as Chloe put her through she would really understand the kids she worked with."

"She would be a great nanny but you would be an even better mom."

"Yeah, someday maybe."

And that was my second missed opportunity because I knew at that moment her mind was on Lila.

"Do you think it will always be so easy between us?"

"I guess it depends in what context you mean. I'm sure we're going to have our share of ups and downs but that just means we'll get to have amazing make-up sex."

"You're such a man! Your mind immediately goes to sex. I guess I just mean that we essentially fell into this relationship and I'm so grateful for it every single day, you have no idea. Aside from a few things we've just sailed through it all. We're in sync with each other, so much so, that sometimes I wonder when the bottom is going to fall out, and once it does, how hard will it be for us to keep it together since we've never had any major problems before?"

I leaned down and kissed the top of her head, pulling her tighter into my arms as we watched the sun go down. She smelled like fresh air and flowers, a scent I would never get enough of.

"Don't worry about stuff like that, Katherine. So far we've been blessed to not have to deal with anything that serious. I was just telling Jessica that we need to keep working on our communication. Talk to me when there's a problem and I'll do the same. If the bottom falls out, I'll always catch you in the end. Just have faith in me, have faith in our love. That's why it's

easy, Katie Grace, because everything we do is surrounded in never ending faith and love."

I should have done it then, that would have been the perfect opportunity, but something about the moment was too serious. I was afraid it would seem like I was proposing in desperation even though it was obviously well planned out. And then, like life, the perfect moment just slipped away and the bottom truly did fall out from under us. I wondered if I were to go back, if she would remember that conversation and still have enough faith in us to let me back in.

I miss her. Being without her for three long years has wreaked havoc on my soul. I can only imagine what it did to her. Katherine was always very sensitive and my harsh words that night could have completely changed her outlook on men and love forever. *I guess that answers my question of going back doesn't it?* I'm just not ready to see how my destruction and despair has changed her. Besides the fact that I don't think I'll ever be ready to hear her say she isn't in love with me anymore. Hearing those words would destroy me.

~~~***~~~

Daniel's lying on his bed, staring up at the ceiling when I get to the house. This is nothing new. Whenever he isn't at work this is how I find him. I've had enough of it already; Vanessa wasn't worth it. He speaks to me but doesn't even turn his head to look at me.

"You smell like the beach."

I chuckle "That's very observant of you. I guess you're relying on your sense of smell lately since you don't seem to be using the rest of them. Let's go get a beer and get you out of this room."

"I'm good, thanks anyway"

So freaking stubborn. "No, you're *not* good. I've got the cavalry on call, one group text and they're all coming over and we're going to have a sit in right here. You have a choice, you can get up and come outside with me and have a beer in Bev's garden OR I send out a text to the masses and your space will be permanently invaded within the hour."

I'm lying through my teeth but he doesn't know that. If I wanted to, all I have to do is send one text and they would all be here. He knows it, too. The last thing he wants is for everyone to show up and invade his space.

"You're a bastard. I've told you that, right?"

"Yup, numerous times, but I'm a bastard with a purpose and right now *you* are my purpose. So we can do this the easy or the hard way. Drink a six pack of Guinness outside with me, or four people will be having a sit in tonight in your room. Your choice."

"At least you got the good beer. Let's go outside."

"I *always* get the good beer *and* I even brought tequila because I love your heartbroken ass so much."

"Tequila first, and I'm not heartbroken. Not exactly, I don't miss Vanessa one bit."

Bev smiles the biggest one I think I've ever seen when we walk through the kitchen, and it gets even bigger when Daniel plants a kiss on her head. She's a smart lady and doesn't say a word as we pass through. She wouldn't want to say anything that would have Daniel heading back to his room.

Out on the table I've got beer, tequila, and In N Out Burgers—all of Daniel's favorites. I'm hoping it will be a good start to get him out of this funk. He ignores the shot glasses and drinks straight from the bottle. *I guess it's going to be one of those nights. It's about time this guy loosens up a bit.*

"So, are you here to psychoanalyze me?"

"Hell no, I'm here to hang out with you, drink with you, and hopefully pull you out of your self-imposed hell."

He lets out a snort. "That's rich coming from you."

"I'll give you that, but my situation is vastly different from yours."

"How so?" *This is definitely going to be one of those nights.* I take the bottle from him and drink, letting the tequila pour down the back of my throat. *Guess I'm staying the night.* We pass the bottle back and forth a few times, sitting in a comfortable silence, before I finally answer him.

"Before I tell you how my situation is different than yours, why don't you tell me what exactly it is that you're upset about?"

"I'm upset about a lot of shit. At the top of the list is being taken advantage of by someone who didn't love me the way I loved her. All I was to her was a fucking payday. It eats at me every day, I second guess everything now. Holy hell, Mike, she wasn't bad when we were together. Other than pushing for the shopping trips she was sweet and kind. How come I couldn't see what was going on right in front of my face?"

"That's a two part answer. The simplest answer is you didn't see it because you're one of the few people in the world that believes in the good in people. You're not jaded by the bad shit that goes on around us day in and day out. The second part of that answer is almost as simple. She didn't *want* you to see her true colors. Vanessa is the definition of a calculated woman. I heard her when she didn't think anyone was around, though, and I know how sweet and nice she was to you. Who knows? Maybe she's got a lot more of that in her than we give her credit for."

"Yeah right."

"I know, but if it's in there, it comes from somewhere. For whatever reason, she wanted to have sex with me and she did everything she could to make sure it happened. I'm still so sorry about that. It's one of my greatest regrets."

"One of them? You have a list or what?"

"You have no idea."

"That's because you don't ever talk. Don't worry about Vanessa, I know you wouldn't do that to me and I know you don't even like her. I'm just always going to be that guy, you know?"

What in the hell is he talking about?

"Enlighten me. What kind of guy?"

Between the two of us, we've already finished the tequila. Daniel pauses a minute, opens a beer, passing me one in the process.

"You know, I'm the nice guy. I'll *always* be the nice guy. The only guy around that believes in good over evil and lets girls walk all over him. I've never thought to look out for the ones who only wanted me for something. I'm a fucking pushover. I'm just done, Mike. No more women for a while, not until I can date one and know she's for real. I'm done. It's your turn to explain your situation."

"Not much to explain. I had the one and it didn't work out. This is the after math. I was the nice guy once, too, and it didn't turn out so well for me. Don't follow the path I took because I don't feel any better when I wake up in the morning now than I did three years ago. The past is a painful place to visit so I don't go there often. I did today and now I'm drinking with you. Someday I'm sure I'll give you more, but for tonight that's all I've got. There are good women out there; Vanessa just wasn't one of them. Don't let yourself stay mad for too long. That shit festers and fills you with poison."

"It's been three years, Mike."

"Yup, like I said, don't follow along my path. You're too good to wallow in misery over a stupid bitch that didn't love you. You've got a bruised ego right now, it'll pass. Just for the record, I know you don't miss her but you miss

the love you gave freely to her. Karma's a bitch
and she'll get hers in the end."

Chapter 14 ~ My Katherine becomes Daniel's Kate

The past few months have been rough. My mom found me and started calling me. She's left me dozens of messages, begging me to call her, letting me know that things weren't actually what she thought. *No shit, I figured that much out pretty fast.* I can't call her yet; I have to talk to Katherine first. It's time. I'm ready.

Daniel finally pulled himself out of his funk and met an amazing woman that makes him happier than I've ever seen him. The same weekend they met was Katherine's birthday weekend. That weekend was the final kick in the ass I needed to talk to Katherine. It came during an epiphany in the form of gardenia perfume that pulled me to my senses.

I'm not complete without her. No matter how many girls I screw, how many drinks I have in order to hide the pain, the only thing that's going to make it better is having her back with me. Daniel convinced me to reach out to her, so I wrote her a letter and now I'm just waiting. Waiting is the worst possible form of evil. I'm so ready to go knock on her door, but I told myself I would give it a week. After the engagement party, I'll be another day closer. Hopefully, she'll call me first and I won't actually have to wait the entire week.

At least I'm getting the chance to meet Connor and Daniel's girlfriends tonight. I'm excited to meet the girls that have nailed both of these guys down at the same time. I'll also get to spend some time with Bev and Rick and Linda and Bryan. It's been a while since I've been able to do that. I was able to get the new deck all finished for Jake before I left earlier today, too. April is going to be over the moon happy when she sees it; she's been begging Jake for months to do something with the yard. I'm just happy I was able to help out and it kept me away from the house last night. As much as I'm looking forward to seeing everyone, I didn't want to be the odd man out. I figure I'll get enough of it at the party, but at least there will be so many people there it won't seem strange. I also need to talk to Ben about finishing up the sleeve on my arm and tonight seems like the perfect time.

I started the sleeve not too long after meeting Daniel. He mentioned he had a buddy who owned a shop and the rest is history. I've been weaving my history with Katherine into the ink on my skin, telling the story of my life through art. It's colorful and destructive, and it probably doesn't make sense to anyone but me, and that's the way I like it. The center of it is the biggest part; it's probably more than half of the entire sleeve. It goes full circle around my arm—an aquatic ocean scene with a sunken boat. Topping the treasure chest in the boat is a replica of the ring I had for Katherine. It's subtle and blends right in with the jewels, but if she sees it she'll know. I've got an amazing one of a catcher's glove falling through mid-air with home plate under it. It's hovering over the plate with a ball caught in the glove but never completes the fall. Ben came up with a great one of a black Mercedes but the hood is a headstone that says R.I.P. Dad. The car is new and shiny but the irony shows through—things can be replaced but people are lost forever. The top part of my arm has a sky scape of the night sky, moon, and stars. The most meaningful of them all is the one that runs across my shoulder and onto my chest. It was the first one I got and simply says *Not all who wander are lost*. It was my own personal reminder that even though I left everything behind to make myself better, it was a choice and not a punishment. That at the end of this journey I *know* where my soul belongs. I still have room for at least one or two more. I've always wanted to really symbolize Katherine (with her knowing this time). Hopefully, someday it could be her name, or our entwined wedding rings, or maybe if I'm lucky, our child's footprints.

From here on out, it's time for new beginnings for me, for my friends, and hopefully for my relationship with Katherine. Tonight will be about fun, and from the looks of this place, we won't be lacking any because it's packed. The valet takes my truck and I enter through the side entrance. As I walk past the guest house, I see Connor walking my way.

"It's about time! Damn, Mike, where have you been? I haven't seen you in weeks."

"I know. With work and everything it's just been crazy. Where's this girl of yours, anyway?" Connor nods his head toward the guest house.

"Jess and Kate are still in there getting ready. Daniel was supposed to bring them up to the house, but either they're running late like girls usually do, or Jess had a fit because I sent Daniel and didn't come and get her myself."

Alarm bells are ringing in my head rapidly. He said Jess and Kate. What are the odds that he and Daniel are dating two UCLA girls with the same but different names of *my* girls? I don't think anyone ever mentioned the name of Connor's girl to me before, and honestly if they did, I didn't pay attention. He changes girls like he changes underwear. *There's no way right?* I'm lost in my thoughts as Connor tries to get my attention, but I see them over his shoulder. I know it's them and I lose my breath. They're gorgeous—the same but different. They're older and all woman, but there's no doubt about it, that's them and they're linked arm in arm with Daniel. They both look happy until they set eyes on me and the bottom falls out of their happily ever after.

~~~***~~~

My worlds have officially collided and not even close to the way I always pictured it happening. Katherine…Kate…is with Daniel. Jessica is with Connor. They actually make a perfect couple; I couldn't have paired either of them up any better.

Daniel threw me daggers all night and he's not the only one. Connor seems pissed at me. Jake tried to corner me to see what was going on, but I'll be damned if I'm going to go against Kate's wishes tonight, so I told him everything was fine and not to worry. He didn't buy it but didn't question it, either. Jake can read me probably better than anyone and he knows something's up. He also knows I'll tell him when I'm ready.

Kate and Daniel went to the guest house a while ago. I know she went to read my letter, but I have no clue what happened after that. Jessica keeps glancing at me, hoping I won't notice, but of course I do. I'm desperate to talk to her and just keep staring at her, hoping she'll give me an opening but she never does.

At least Ben and Callie felt the uncomfortable vibe and excused themselves to dance. Jessica and Connor have had their heads bent together, talking for the last five minutes or so, and all I can do is sit here and nurse my drink. I told her in the letter I would respect her relationship if she had one. How can I do that? How can I sit back and watch her and Daniel together? It's physically impossible; I *can't* do it. She's *mine*.

Daniel walks back to the table alone, head hanging and tie undone, with an aura of sadness surrounding him. He doesn't look at me and I don't blame him; I can't make eye contact with him right now, either.

"Daniel, where's Kate?" I hear the panicked tone in Jess's voice matching the feeling I have in my heart.

"She left," he answers dejectedly

"What the hell, man? You let her leave? We've got to go get her. She can't be alone right now." Connor jumps up, running his hands through his hair.

"She read Mike's letter and she begged me to let her go. We're all supposed to be at her house by nine in the morning. She said she wouldn't make any decisions without talking it through, but I guess we'll see. Can you guys take me to my house to get my truck? If it's all the same to you, I'd rather stay at your house tonight, Connor."

"Yeah sure, let's go give our excuses and get out of here. Jess, wait here, okay? You're crying and I don't want to make a big scene." She nods at him and pulls a tissue from her clutch.

"Jessica, I…I'm sorry. There's so much I want to say to you but it all seems insignificant somehow right now."

She sniffs and wipes her nose with the tissue, finally looking me in the eye for the first time. Instead of the anger that was there a few hours ago, her eyes are filled with utter sadness.

"Michael, I honestly don't know what to say to you. I've missed you and I'm pissed at you and I'm so fucking relieved to see you. I've been so worried about you, wondering if you were ever going to come back to us. Did you ever think about us? About Kate? About me?"

"Every single day, Jess, and every single night. I just wasn't ready to face her, or you. How do you single handedly shatter your very own existence and then come back and try to piece it back together? When I destroyed my life I broke her trust, I broke your trust, and I don't know if I can ever get it back. But it's the one thing I want more than anything in this world."

"He loves her, Mike, with his whole heart."

Her voice catches when she says that, almost like it tears her up to have to tell me. I understand the feeling completely because my voice probably sounds the same when I answer her.

"I know he does. Does she love him?" I ask the question that I never want to know the answer to.

"She does, but it's not that black and white with her, even if she doesn't realize that. She's not the same girl you left behind, Mike. This was a long, sad journey we took to get her here. Kate has things she'll have to tell you herself, and until she does, until she heals her heart, I don't know if she'll ever be able to fully give it to anyone. Even if she thinks she has."

While I'm absorbing her words and trying to process their cryptic meaning, Daniel and Connor come back.

"Alright, we told everyone Kate had to go home and help with Lauren. Let's get out of here. You too, Mike. We're all staying at my house tonight."

Daniel doesn't look happy but he nods, "Kate wants all of us there in the morning, it makes sense."

I follow them all the way back to Kate's house. The entire drive was a blur of memories and thoughts. I spent most of the drive trying to figure out if there was a point in the last two weeks where I could have pieced this puzzle together sooner but there wasn't. All nicknames, no last names. I haven't talked to Connor in forever, but maybe if I had I would have figured it out.

He's had her for two weeks, but I had her for over ten years. Will she really pick him over me? *Fuck! I hate this. Tomorrow can't come soon enough.* We pull up to the girls' house all at the same time, Daniel and I jumping out of our trucks in a race to find Kate. As soon as Jess opens the garage, we're painfully aware Kate isn't here.

Jess pulls out her phone and rapidly scrolls through her text messages. "The last text she sent says she was going to the gym. Marc's gym isn't in the best area, and this time of night she'll be alone. Connor, can you please go and check on her?"

"Sure, angel, text me the address. Keep an eye on these two while I'm gone and make sure they don't do anything stupid."

I'm still fuming from hearing she's with Marc to pay too much attention to Connor. I lean up against my truck and nail Jessica with a gaze.

"She's still hanging out with Marc? For the love all that is holy, why hasn't that son of a bitch fallen off a cliff yet?"

Jessica actually laughs at that, and as pissed off as I am, it's really nice to see her smile. "Mike, you've missed a lot. Kate and Marc are really close. Had you stuck around, you probably could've hindered that growth, but now they're thick as thieves. She's probably over there filling him in on all of tonight's developments and asking for advice."

If I said all the expletives out loud that are running through my head right now they would think I'm crazy. I guess time hasn't changed my feelings for Marc except making my dislike for him even stronger.

"Why do you care, Mike? You've been out of the picture for almost four years. She's my girlfriend, and if it doesn't bother me it shouldn't bother you."

Oh hell no. I'm so worked up right now I don't even care if he's my best friend.

"What's it to *me*? I'll tell you, Daniel. Marc wants to fuck Kate, and if he hasn't done it yet, it's still the first thing on his agenda, *guaranteed*. He's a piece of shit that has wanted in her pants since he was old enough to know what fucking was. If you love *your* girlfriend so much maybe it *should* bother you!" By now I'm up in his face, fists clenched at my side. I can't believe he doesn't care.

"Enough, you two, we've had enough drama for one night, don't you think? Listen, this isn't going to resolve anytime soon, so why don't you each take separate corners in your trucks. I'm not in the mood to monitor a pissing match tonight and I think you both should do yourselves a favor and keep your distance from each other until *after* you talk to Kate tomorrow. Deal?"

"Deal," we reply in unison

Finally, Connor texts us and tells us to go back to his house and he'll meet us there in a bit after he stops by to say goodnight to Jess. We let ourselves in, not saying a word, but the look in

Daniels eyes tells me he has so much he wants to say and I'm sure he gets a similar feeling from me. I don't want to get hurt and I don't want to hurt him, either. This situation is probably as bad as it can get and nothing short of a miracle is going to fix it.

Finally, Connor comes in and chooses to talk to Daniel first, which is understandable. They have been friends longer and Kate is technically his girlfriend at the moment. Then he comes and talks to me.

"She's fine. She was with Marc working some things out. I know you don't like him, but you're going to have to deal with that and a lot more right now."

He's frustrated and I can tell he wants to lay into me.

"I know I will."

"Look, Mike, this situation is so much more complex than you could ever imagine. I need you to understand something, though. Kate is my sister. I would lay down my life to protect her. Tread lightly with how you proceed. Not only is her mental state on the line, but her whole heart is very delicate. It's taken her a very long time to try and let go of her past enough to move forward with her future. Don't fuck this up for her."

"She's not the only one that has to deal with the past, Connor. You can't tell me you've been immune to my life the past few years. I've obviously been trying to forget about the past. It's cool, though, you need to take sides in this and protect Kate and Daniel. I get it, no hard feelings."

"Fuck you, Mike, this is bigger than that! And yes, I'll protect Kate, Daniel, and Jess, but at the end of the day I want to protect you, too! Don't mistake my anger for more than what it is. You could've avoided this whole thing by telling us your story a long time ago. You run from *everything*! They met *on* Kate's birthday. Let me guess…that is the *exact* reason you ran to Vegas…because it was her birthday and it would have been too tempting to drink your problems away here. I get you, Mike, even if you think I don't."

"Did she talk about me, Connor? After you met, did she ever mention our relationship?"

"It's not my place to get into this with you. Look, Kate, talked about you vaguely but it wasn't until the past few weeks I really heard the whole story about you throwing the ring at her and the nasty things you said. I shouldn't even tell you this much but I think I need to. Tomorrow, Kate is going to talk to you, and you're going to learn things that exceed *anything* you could have imagined. Whatever you guys decide to do, however you decide to pick up and move on, I'll support her decisions."

"Fair enough. Thanks, man."

Connor yawns, and in turn so do I. "Oh, by the way, Kate wants you to bring bagels and o.j. in the morning. Goodnight, Mike."

"Night, Connor."

A new day

I've been up all night and I'm not even tired. My brain has been working overtime remembering everything that Kate and I have been through in our lives. Not just her but all of us. I thought going back to those places in my mind that I haven't visited in a while would give me some form of clarity so that I could make Daniel realize that Kate and I are meant to be.

Instead, what I've learned is that what I thought was so black and white is actually filled with shades of grey. The past four years have been filled with love and heartache, but they have also been filled with amazing friendships and family. I was saved by my new family and I've become the man that I am because of them and their strength and love.

I still want Kate, and I will have her back in my arms soon, hopefully with Daniel's blessing. This time, instead of rushing out and making life altering decisions, I'm taking stock of all that I've gained and all I have to lose. My life is graced with amazing people and I don't want to lose them. I realize I need to take this slowly. I'll still explain my story to Daniel, but first I'm going to talk to Jake. If there's anyone that can help me work through this, with any chance of still hanging on to my friends and family, it's him.

I've got nothing but time right now, and I don't need to push Kate or try and force her into anything more than friendship. I need to earn back her love and respect and remind her every day in subtle ways why it was that she fell in love with me to begin with. I broke her heart and it's only fair that I try and put it back together with love, one piece at a time.

Kate's journey continues in Releasing Kate, Book Two of The Acceptance Series coming Winter 2014

Keep reading for an excerpt

Endless gratitude pages

Usually this is called the thank you page, but sometimes thank you just doesn't seem like enough. Endless gratitude seems more appropriate because you all have mine.

D's Divine Divas – You know who you are and I love each and every one of you. You aren't just my street team, you are my friends. You are my sombrero wearing, pickle pimping, Friday night storytelling, Vegas troublemaking, margarita drinking, author pimping, rock stars! You give me so much more than you will ever know and that's where the endless gratitude comes in. I could never thank you enough for your inspiration, friendship, love, and support. I can't wait until we take Vegas by storm!

My family – you've got my gratitude now and always. Thank you for your unwavering faith in me. I know I'm difficult and can be bitchy at times and you still love me in spite of my issues. Your love is priceless. I'm so blessed that you belong to me.

My beta readers – Heidi, Ashley, Nadine, Mandy, and Caterina ~ You guys…there just are no words. GRATITUDE and so much of it to you all. Your suggestions and lack of sugar coating things are why we have a book. You know I like it straight up and you never fail to tell me "Hey, bitch, that sucks ass." Maybe in nicer words, but that's usually the bottom line and I wouldn't have it any other way.

Tiffany Tillman – My amazing editor that understands all too well how much life gets in the way of deadlines. Much Gratitude to you, girl! We always make it work even when the odds are against us; I think that says something for our spirit and determination.

Regina Wamba – My beautifully creative cover designer. I could never show you the amount of GRATITUDE I have for you. Before anyone reads the pages, the book sings to them through the cover that you create! WE are all so blessed that your creative heart makes our books into art. To top it all off, you are a beautiful soul inside and out and that just flows into everything you do. You're amazing!

There are a few people that just go above and beyond for me and I have to give my endless gratitude to them. Ashley Griffieth, Heidi Ryan, Kristi Widner Collins, Suzi White, Ashley Hampton, Stracey Charran, Carol Ray, Loca Crzn, Cindy Baker, and Caterina Ayala. Love you girls so HARD!

My amazing friends that push me even when I have no motivation to get there, you know who you are. MAK, CAT, and KJD, more than gratitude you have my love. Xoxo

My readers. OMG I still can't believe I get to type that! You guys are amazing. I love the emails and posts in the discussion group. I still can't get over how invested you all are in my characters, especially those of you that have picked your teams and are in it for the long haul. I know how hard it is to give an author your faith, especially a new one who writes a series that you have to read to the end. I hope I continue to do you all proud. Please know how much your emails and reviews mean to me. The fact that you take the time to reach out and voice your opinion is priceless. Those of you in my discussion group and street team, know that I love interacting with and getting to know you all. Please consider leaving a review if you haven't already, even if the book wasn't your cup of tea. Constructive, negative, and positive reviews help authors grow. You guys have my endless gratitude, you invest your time into my books, and to me that is one of the greatest blessings. #TeamKate #TeamDaniel #TeamMike #TeamConnor #TeamApril #TeamJake or even #TeamMarc, thanks for choosing a side. #TeamUndecided, thanks for keeping an open mind.

There are so many authors and bloggers that have supported me, allowed me to take over their pages, and given me amazing advice. I couldn't possibly mention you all and I don't want to leave any of you out. Just know that if you've helped me, guided me, promoted my books, let me take over your blog, shared in my highs and lows, or just chatted with me, I love you all and am eternally grateful to have you in my life. Our jobs aren't always easy—there's a lot of blood, sweat, and tears that go into being a blogger or an author. Keeping your head up, staying away from drama, and being positive isn't always easy to do, and yet most of you do it with grace and style. ETERNAL GRATITUDE to you all for being great examples to follow.

To my two favorite receptionists at my favorite NS office, you girls make my day whenever I come for a visit. That's not always an easy feat when I typically have a raging migraine. Gratitude to you both.

If I forgot anyone that knows they should have been here, I'm sorry; I have the most forgetful mind. It wasn't intentional, I promise. I love you just as much as I always have.

Thank you all for taking this journey with me. I'm so very blessed to be taking it with all of you. My life has been enriched in ways I never thought possible. Thank you for reading my books and being in my life.

XOXO~

Dee

For those of you who have read my books I know many of you feel strongly about #TeamDaniel and #TeamMike. Your feedback, ratings, and reviews are very important to independent authors. Please leave a rating and consider leaving a review, I'd love to hear your thoughts.

Feel free to visit:

My website ~ http://www.dkellyauthor.com

My Facebook page ~ https://www.facebook.com/dkellyauthor

Google + ~ https://plus.google.com/+DeeKellyAuthor/posts

Twitter ~ https://twitter.com/dkellyauthor

Goodreads ~ https://www.goodreads.com/author/show/7492436 .D_Kelly

Pinterest ~ http://www.pinterest.com/deekellyauthor/

Stay up to date on all current news, new releases, and giveaways by joining my mailing list ~

http://www.dkellyauthor.com/mailing-list

Feel free to drop me an email at ~ dkellyauthor@gmail.com

Excerpt from Releasing Kate

Book two of The Acceptance Series

Connor – Six weeks later

"Don't, Connor, just DON'T! Kate is my best friend, my fucking sister, but she is out of her ever loving, god damn mind! What the hell was she thinking tonight? She just crossed the most uncrossable line, and of course there was no reasoning with her because she was so damn drunk."

I watch her anger slowly dissipate into sadness, just like it has for the past few weeks every time she gets worked up over Kate and her situation. "I know, Jess, trust me, but put yourself in her shoes for a minute, angel. How would you be acting if the two loves of your life were suddenly off limits to you? I'll admit, alcohol isn't the answer, but for the first time in weeks she looked like she was taking her mind off of things. She was having a good time; she almost looked like our Kate again. With all the chaos in her life right now, that is a good thing. Whatever the repercussions are for her actions, she'll have to deal with them. Before we judge her, we need to assume she knows what she was doing and why. Our girl is heartbroken with a capital H, and all else aside, we just have to be there for her when she finally succumbs to the pain and falls. Unfortunately, I think that is going to be sooner rather than later but maybe that's a good thing. Once she breaks and lets it all out, only then will she begin to heal."

Taking her hand into mine, I pull her into a tight embrace. We hold each other in desperation, as if our lives depend on it. Both of us are shrouded in sadness and longing. In the last few weeks, we haven't had a whole lot of time for ourselves. Instead, we've been managing our friends, trying to keep them sane and from inflicting bodily harm on each other. I miss having alone time with my girl. Hell, I miss having sex-a-thons with my girl. I make a mental note to find a way to change that real soon.

"Go upstairs and take a nice relaxing bath. I'll wait up for Katie down here and talk her off the ledge when she gets home, if she gets home. Besides, you're way too worked up to talk to her gently and I don't think she can handle more than a gentle discussion, not after tonight."

Jess sighs into my chest, clutching onto my shirt extra tight as her tears start to fall. I brush them aside tenderly with my fingers and tilt her head up so I can kiss away her tears. It kills me when she cries, and she's been crying a lot lately.

"I just… I just… damn, Connor, I just love her so fucking much, you know? She was happy. For the first time in years she was my Kate again. There was light in her eyes, happiness in her laugh, and so much love in her heart. I'm losing her slowly this time and it's worse than before. I can't put my finger on it. From what I can see, she's self-destructing. None of us are going to come out of this unscathed. I'm exhausted and my feet hurt so I'm going to take you up on your offer to stay up and deal with her. I know I won't be any help tonight. Just don't stay up too late, okay? I have a feeling her bed isn't going to be slept in." Jess gives me a whisper of a kiss, and instead of those fuck me heels she had on all night being wrapped around my neck, they're now in her hands as she drags herself up the stairs.

When did our happy group become the biggest episode of Dawson's Creek ever written? Yes, I went there, don't judge. April made us watch the whole damn series with her when she had her tonsils out. However, in our version of the creek I would be the straight version of Jack. I guess that makes Kate our resident Joey, Mike would be Dawson, and Daniel would be Pacey. On the show, where Pacey clearly violated every rule known to man by stealing his best friend's girl, it's the flipside over here. In our creek, Dawson, aka Mike, is clearly in the wrong. He gave up any and all rights to Kate when he stormed out of her life four years ago, never to return. Daniel is devastated but pushing through and Jake has taken Mike's side in all of it which makes things difficult. I'm trying to stay neutral. I love them, but my priority is Kate. In their defense, they are trying to be amicable in front of Kate and trying not to let her see how turbulent things really are between them. Thank god for that because that is the last thing she needs to worry about. They need to work that shit out themselves and leave her out of it. This isn't on Kate's shoulders—it shouldn't be—this whole mess is between them. While Kate is being the strong one, the moral one, the one standing up for family, and for friendship, they're being pig-headed assholes in the midst of the biggest pissing match I have ever seen. They're all hurting and will likely continue to do so until after the baby comes, and then who knows what will happen.

I can see it in Kate's eyes, though. She won't admit it but she's in love with them both. After hearing about her past with Mike and knowing how her fairytale with Daniel started, I can see why. I wouldn't want to be in her shoes, it's an impossible decision. I actually think she did the right thing by removing herself from the equation. I know who she belongs with, who her heart leans to. I can hear it when she speaks, see it in her expressions. But tonight she took the path unchosen. The one that might lead her to temporary bliss, but it's going to leave a trail of destruction in its wake. She essentially opened Pandora's Box. Let's just pray when it's all said and done that hope still remains in the bottom of the box

Made in the USA
Las Vegas, NV
27 December 2021